Sharad P. Paul

PICADOR

First published 2007 by Picador
an imprint of Pan Macmillan Ltd
Pan Macmillan, 20 New Wharf Road, London N1 9RR
Basingstoke and Oxford
Associated companies throughout the world
www.panmacmillan.com

ISBN 978-0-330-45147-5

Printed in India by Gopsons Papers Ltd, Noida

Sharad P. Paul was born in England, grew up in India and has lived in New Zealand since 1991. After residencies in both Family Medicine and Plastic Surgery, he entered medical practice. He also has a Law degree and holds a Masters in Medical Law from the University of Glasgow. He lives in Auckland, New Zealand, where he owns the bookstore Baci. This is his first novel.

For Natasha, my daughter.
Sweetheart, one day you will be old enough to
read this story and won't have to sneak peeks
while I am writing.

With particular thanks to:

My agent Glenys Bean, without whom this book
would not be published.

Mike Wagg, for being a picky and thorough
proofreader.

Picador editors Shruti Debi and Sam Humphreys for
believing in this novel.

My family, for their unconditional love and support.

This story is dedicated to that ancient beautiful language, Tamil, and to the seventy million Tamil-speaking people worldwide. I have seen the love of language ease their sorrows and hardship, attenuate mistakes and irritations; Tamil patois fills everyday life with wonderful stories. I have penned some of these stories in this book.

This novel has nine chapters.

The number 9 symbolises the union of the male and the female; 9 is neither masculine nor feminine – it is the number, the mark of the ali: *the eunuch*

– Tamil saying

Contents

1. Cool Cut – the beginning   1

2. The kite flyers   18

3. Descent into nightmares   37

4. Kumar and Lakshmi – the union   54

5. The wedding   71

6. Eunuch life   91

7. Kumar and Lakshmi – the reunion   109

8. The escape   125

9. Cool Cut – the end   144

COOL CUT reads the sign outside Kumar's barber shop. Kumar is my favourite barber. I've already been waiting for a quarter of an hour for my haircut. I try to avoid the gaze of the second barber. He usually cuts hair in chair no. 2. I try to not let him know that I don't want him to cut my hair. It is the right thing to do, for me. After all, I only get my hair cut once a month.

I admit I am a bit vain. It is Patti's fault. I really need glasses. Mum and Dad are willing to take me to the shop to get a pair of spectacles. But I don't like glasses. Kids who wear them end up with small eyes. And other kids call them 'soda bottle' eyes. However, Patti hears that I might need to wear glasses and won't allow that to happen to me.

Now, she is not really my grandmother, although everyone calls her Patti, which means 'grandmother' in Tamil. She sits outside on the porch of her house, grinding her toothless gums. Every time I pass by she smiles a toothless smile. Her sagging breasts hang down to her waist, peeping outside the folds of her white sari. Her husband died many years ago. He was a big drinker. Dad says his liver got cooked. In accordance with the local rural farming Gounder caste tradition, a widow is not allowed to wear coloured clothing. Patti is also not allowed to wear a blouse under her white sari to restrain her pendulous breasts. People say tight blouses make women attractive and marriageable.

'How old are you, Patti?' I ask her.

'Probably thirty.'

'Thirty! You can't be thirty! My Dad's older than that!'

'OK, maybe thirty-five then,' she says, giving me a toothless grin.

I think that is all she can count up to. But Dad says that as old folk have never had a date of birth recorded, they think they are all 'probably thirty' years old.

'You have such a sweet face, which will be positively ruined by glasses,' she declares with the authority of her 'probably thirty' years. Her opinion prevails. Although I struggle to see things very far away, I don't object to being considered a 'sweet face'. A sweet face needs a cool haircut, I reckon.

It is the summer of 1975. It is hot in Madras. It is always hot in Madras.

Cool Cut has an air conditioner. The breeze from the machine makes the air cool. On the wall is a large portrait of MGR.

MGR is the Marlon Brando of Tamil movies – a legend amongst ordinary actors. He is also big in politics. The speaker next to me plays music from the movie *Utthaman (The Innocent)*. I remember that movie – especially the scene where MGR heroically saves the life of the frostbitten heroine by warming her up; he warms her up by making love to her. I hum along to the tune.

On the opposite wall is a kite. It is diamond-shaped and made out of old newspapers. I try to read the date on the newspaper, but the letters are too far away. Or my eyes are too weak. I can see bold red letters emblazoned across the face of the kite. They read 'I LOVE YOU'.

I can see the eyes of the barber in chair no. 2 looking at me.

'Are you waiting for a haircut or a shave?' he asks.

'Don't you need a rest?' I say.

'Are you out of your mind? If you mess with me, I will knock your teeth out one by one and count them.'

I stammer that I am waiting for Kumar, the main barber. Over the drone of the air conditioner, I can hear barber no. 2 cross the floor and leave the room. I know he is angry.

I have got myself into a difficult situation, but my looks come first.

Chair no. 1 is free. Kumar beckons me with a nod of his head. I sit down. He covers me with a red plastic drape. I sneeze as he sprays my hair with a fine mist of water. There is a large mirror in front of us, covering the whole wall. I can see the other barber sitting in the back room. Kumar says the other barber is pissed off; pissed off like a hooker in a brothel line-up when a man picks another girl, he says.

Kumar looks at my hair critically, 'You've left it too long this time.'

He gets his scissors and begins to cut my hair. His fingers grab clumps of my hair, wildly and urgently, and he snips away. He is an image of total concentration. There is a perfectly good reason for that. There is no better reason than one's looks, he says.

I listen to his stories. Kumar says that, in ancient times, barbers were the storytellers to the maharajas. Every day the maharaja would ask for two stories, while the barber shaved his beard. The first story was usually true and about the kingdom. The second story was usually made up by the barber.

Today, he tells me about kites. Paper kites know how to float on the air, he says. They can do serious stuff without wings; like dreams. Kumar's stories

4

usually make me feel important. I feel like an old maharaja. He tells me stories as if I am his age. I push my chest out and sit straight. My muscles look stronger.

'Keep still,' he commands. 'What are you doing these days?'

'Still finishing school,' I answer. 'This is my last year at school.'

MGR looks down at me from his portrait. Kumar mops my brow, picks hair off my forehead and continues cutting my hair. He sees me looking up at MGR.

'Except MGR, all politicians are crooks,' he says. 'You had better not vote for the DMK,' he warns. 'MGR is God. Granted, he may not be *the* god, but he is *a* god, nonetheless. Make sure you vote for the ADMK: MGR's party.'

'Who is in charge of the DMK?' I inquire seriously.

'Karunanidhi – he's too corrupt. What sort of a man names his son *Stalin?*'

These are important times in Madras. The central government of India has made the learning of Hindi language compulsory. Hindi is being pushed as the new national language.

Everyone has to learn Hindi in school until fifth grade. Around here, many kids go to work even if they have not been to school. They can all read and write Tamil, which is their mother tongue. People are intimidated by Hindi. Government officials are making many signs change to the Hindi alphabet. I can read Hindi because I learnt it at school, but I don't speak it. I don't *want* to speak it. I can perhaps muster up a dialect but not proper spoken Hindi. I write in Tamil because it is a poetic language. Kumar says we dream in Tamil because it is a very quiet language. It lingers in the background of our dreams, never threatening to overwhelm our imagination; unlike Hindi. Hindi is noise. Hindi can be used to describe what happens every day, but you cannot dream in Hindi.

Kumar is right. This is Madras – the bustling capital of the state of Tamil Nadu (which translates to 'Tamil Country'). This is the home of the Dravidian people who were here before the Aryans established the Indus Valley Civilization 4,000 years ago. It is absurd that a language you cannot dream in can become a national language.

Riots have broken out in the streets. There has been unrest for years, but it has now erupted like molten lava. Buses are being burnt. The radio informs us that it is bus no. 93C that has been torched. A cinema which dared screen a Hindi movie has just been firebombed. Signposts in Hindi are being tarred black.

Kumar says, 'We shouldn't have to speak or learn Hindi.'

I agree. To speak Hindi we have to study it. It is like seeing postcards of America without going there. You see cowboys, Disneyland and pictures of the Red Indian people – even if just the ones that were not killed off by the white men. I am a Dravidian, from the south of India. I am descended from the aboriginal people of the south of India. My roots are here. I have tried to learn Hindi but the words won't form in my mouth. I don't want the prime minister to say, 'Good. You are learning the national language.' That will be like being unfaithful to Tamil. I think many people like me will live in Tamil and die in Hindi. Hindi is an unapproachable, ungrateful language.

Outside in the street I hear the rush of an oncoming bus. There are a lot of buses today. People come from the villages to hear MGR. He is going to speak at a political rally. He is leading the battle against the Hindi imposition. The radio keeps us informed of the progress of MGR's motorcade.

My hair is finally done and Kumar inspects my stubble. Until today he has run a clipper over my chin, after my haircut. That has been our ritual for the past three years.

'Time for your first shave,' he declares.

I feel like a big man. I wonder if I should ask my father first. Big men don't ask their fathers. 'Do I get the lather and everything?'

'You bet.' Kumar beams and whips out a gleaming knife. I turn my face to my left side and the cold metal presses against my cheek. One must always shave the left cheek first. Shaving the right side first brings bad luck, Kumar says.

'Maybe I should have the clippers,' I stammer.

'Nonsense, a good shave is the essence of a gentleman.'

I look up. On the ceiling I see the motto of Cool Cut painted in bright red letters – 'GOD MADE MAN BUT COOL CUT MADE HIM GENTLEMAN'.

I am almost one now. I smile nervously. I lean back and Kumar layers cream on my cheeks. He works up the lather with a brush. Mounds of cumulus flow from his brush, while he steadies my head with a melange of gentleness and warmth. I stop talking as he nears my throat. He can't concentrate on the contours of the cumulus if I keep talking, I reason. It might be dangerous.

'Shaving foam looks like a cloud,' he says, reading my mind.

Dreams belong in the clouds. Anything else among the clouds, like airplanes, doves, storks, eagles is too intrusive. They push thoughts in wrong directions. Except dreams and kites, he says.

'Kites?' I ask.

'I love kites. In fact, I more than love them – they are my passion. Someday, I will tell you a story about kites,' he says.

He used to be a kite-flying champion, he says.

I walk out into the street. Walking out of the cool barber shop into the bright furnace of the midday sun sears my skin. The roads are teeming with people. Every street, designed two centuries ago by the British with specific purpose, is now rendered useless by the teeming masses. Intrigued and moved by this river of humanity, I walk towards the function ground.

I realise that I forgot to ask Kumar about the kite on the wall.

The crowd chants 'MGR, MGR' in anticipation of his arrival. They are like a choir, longing for the visitation of an angel. I hear stories of how good-looking MGR is. A woman on my left tells her friend, 'MGR is so fair because he eats gold *basmam* every day.' Wow! MGR eats gold flakes like I eat rice flakes for breakfast! The conversation then goes from his consumption of gold on to his movies.

MGR will deliver us from Hindi, people say. He will rally the whole state to stage a mighty strike, and even the central government will have to take notice.

Isn't MGR from Kerala? I want to ask. I have more sense than that. I know MGR is not a Tamil, although he is the biggest Tamil movie star.

MGR is here. He looks different from the MGR I have seen in the shadows of the movies. He seems starker than his legend. His skin is white and smooth like porcelain. Must be all the gold he eats. He walks on to the hastily rigged platform, wearing his trademark sunglasses.

I have heard amazing stories of MGR's speeches, and his special rapport with women. But this is the real deal.

MGR raises his right hand. '*Thaikulame!* (invoking all mothers in the audience) *Rathathin rathame* (my blood of blood)!' he thunders.

The crowd cheers, all raising their right hands to show the blood flowing in their veins.

He knows the language of women, especially mothers – a language of justice and freedom, he says. He speaks of all the things that women have always been silent about. He speaks of Dravidian women, with their immeasurable hospitality, their powers of redemption, their gifts of healing and their inner fire. MGR says the most powerful beings are Tamil women – women with the inner fire. After all, did not Kannagi burn the whole of Madurai down with the flame of her anger, when her husband was wrongfully accused?

'Do not underestimate the fire in our women,' he lets the central government know. 'Hindi will have no chance in Tamil Nadu.'

I look around me. The crowd has trebled. Where have all these faces come from? There are farmers, labourers, policemen, fishermen and, of course, thousands of women. They look at MGR through flaming eyes, as if in a trance. A floodlight is turned on and anoints the crowd in a yellow glow. It lights up the turmeric which Tamil women use on their skin, the incandescence almost setting them alight. There are a thousand Kannagis willing to burn down cities right here, for the Tamil cause.

I catch a word here and there, but most of his speech is drowned out by the crowd. The crowd keeps shouting *Puratchi Thalaiver* ('Revolutionary Leader'), again and again.

Women surge forward, carrying their babies aloft for MGR to bless them. He picks up the little ones and raises them up high – high enough to reach the smiles of the gods, he says. He is smiling. Kumar is right. MGR *is* different. Now the speakers blare songs from MGR's movies. I feel like rushing back to tell Kumar but Cool Cut seems an island distant from this sea of people.

People are now dancing to the music. There are dark faces, fair faces, faces with perfect features, faces with incomplete features; all dancing like spirits to MGR's movie songs.

I see fireworks lighting up the sky with coloured lights and effusive gleams.

'Isn't he beautiful?' a woman exclaims. I look towards the stage. I can make out MGR's face, although it is a shadow. In the brilliance of the fireworks his face glows like twilight. Women shout in ecstasy, emboldened by the thrill of pure intoxication. I am standing with the women as there are separate sections for men and women. Children are lucky – they get to choose. I have had my first shave today. I wonder if I will be asked to go and stand with the men. I like standing among the women, though. It makes me go a bit tingly. No one takes note of me.

Then one woman sniffs the air while dancing, saying that she can smell something burning. I can't smell anything. Mother always says that women's noses can smell better than men's noses. Then I see a fire; two fires, actually. Two young men have just poured kerosene on themselves and set themselves aflame. It happens at every meeting, a woman near me informs me proudly. Two men burn themselves at every MGR meeting. Seeing him in the flesh overwhelms them, she says. Most other politicians or film stars in Madras would be lucky to have one man kill himself in their honour, in a hundred years. MGR has the highest kill ratio, she says. That is the hallmark of a Tamil superstar.

The crowd stands by and watches while the men burn. No one does anything to stop the men in their mission. Finally, policemen arrive. They have to club a few people with their wooden lathis to clear a path through the curious milling crowd. One of the policemen tries to douse the flame with his bare hands. Another pours buckets of water on the young men. While the policemen try to subdue the flames, every hot spot they extinguish on the men seems to flare up in anger again. It is as if fate (and kerosene) is determined to prevent the policemen from reducing MGR's kill ratio. Newer hot spots light up on the men's bodies in defiance, and the policemen are not successful.

The crowd stands by, in silence. I get the feeling that MGR makes ordinary things become more than ordinary. I see him on the stage, still talking, the floodlights reflected on his dark glasses. His woollen 'Gandhi' cap sits firmly on his head. 'Look at him,' a voice cries, 'he does not look a day over forty and he has acted in over four hundred films!' There are more cheers. I'm standing there lost in thought when the loudspeaker announces that MGR will be leaving soon to another meeting. MGR waves goodbye. 'You are all smart people. I never have to tell you whom to vote for,' he says. The crowd waves goodbye to MGR. I think they respect each other.

MGR's car has stalled. Someone says it has run out of fuel. The driver steps out of the car, his head bowed. He is ashamed. He averts his face from the crowd, fearing for his life. He has let MGR down. He has let the crowd down. He has let the whole state of Tamil Nadu down.

The policemen spring into action, rushing away to get fuel. Petrol sells for seven rupees a litre. Petrol here is illegally mixed with kerosene, Dad says. That is why the vehicles belch black smoke. Some lorries belch such black smoke that one can't see through it.

'MGR's car needs pure fuel, not adulterated crap,' someone shouts. The police jeep rushes towards the airport to bring aircraft fuel. Jet fuel is not adulterated. It sells for forty-five rupees a litre. People are tight-fisted here, except when it comes to gods. I remember Kumar telling me that MGR is a god. I guess a god cannot be driven on a chariot with normal fuel. The aircraft fuel arrives. I see a policeman put the large drum on the ground. He then sucks into a pipe and closes the end with his finger. He puts the end into the fuel tank and lets go of his finger. Fuel begins to enter the tank.

'What is he doing?' I ask.

'Siphoning, you idiot!' someone calls out. My face turns red.

The crowd cheers as fuel flows into the tank.

'The pleasure is ready!' someone yells.

My teacher says that when cars were first introduced in the West, people called them 'pleasure cars'. She sometimes shows us a picture of a 1950 'Chevrolet Motoring Pleasure Car' advertisement from America.

In Tamil a motor car stills translates into *magizhundhuvandi* – 'pleasure car'. Sometimes people shorten it to just 'pleasure'. Tamil language understands the dreams of men. Men get excited about cars. Cars give men pleasure. Why *not* call a car a pleasure? MGR's pleasure is fuelled and ready to leave. People gather around as it begins to move slowly. Some run alongside the car, trying to hold on to the bumpers at the back. 'There might be a space between us,' says MGR, in his usual raspy low voice, as if a spirit is speaking out of him, 'but there will never be a space between our hearts.' The crowd swoons with acute comprehension and happiness. It is time for MGR to depart. I realise it is time for me to depart too.

I can see the curved top of MGR's Ambassador car leaving, the sound diminishing. There is relief from the noise of the crowd. I can see MGR's woollen cap through the back window of his pleasure. That scene, isolated and momentary, shall live in my mind for eternity. Now the car is in the distance. No one trails the car now, except for silence. I am almost home. I drift slowly through the park, finally reaching our house. I can see Father through a bedroom window, completing a newspaper crossword.

Mother comes rushing out. 'Where were you? I was getting worried.'

I tell Mother and Father I was at MGR's speech.

'Amma, his skin was so fair and perfect.'

'That is because he eats gold basmam,' she says.

'That is because he can *afford* to eat gold,' says Father, crustily.

'Your hair is too short in the front,' says Mum. She thinks it will make my face look bigger. She inspects my chin. 'Look, he has been shaved. My baby is no longer a baby!' She has tears flowing down her face. Mothers can be silly like that.

I am finally in bed.

'You were a bit snappy about MGR,' Mum whispers to Dad. Mum and Dad think I am asleep.

'Why should *I* care about how he looks?'

'You know, our neighbour, Pratima told me that she went to see *Utthaman*. In the scene where MGR is disrobing, his thighs were beautifully white. She told me she thinks his cock will be nice and rosy and not like her husband's black baby cobra.'

'Shhh. Our son might still be awake.'

He is; I am. I smile a tired smile. The night is unusually chilly, and my sleep will be broken. It has been a day of highs. MGR is an exception in a universe of boring politics, even to my youthful mind. Finally, my eyelids hide away the remembrance and the knowledge of the day.

2

NEAR SALEM, in the southern Indian state of Tamil Nadu, the Kaveri River flows through a narrow gorge. On the banks of this gorge there is a tiny village called KKP. Now, this seems a bizarre name for a village, and no one knows the origins of this name. It is thought that it originates from the initials of a local British secretary in the final days of the Raj – K. K. Pickering. Others feel that it is just an acronym for *ka ka pee*, which means 'crow shit' in Tamil. It is in this village that Kumar's story begins.

Kumar's father has given him a kite. Kumar runs his hand over the rough paper. 'There is a right way and a wrong way to release the kite,' Father explains. 'Tomorrow I will show you.' Kumar's father shows Kumar how to hold the rope and gently release the kite. One must let the kite take off gently, until it is above all the treetops. It is best to learn to fly the kite at night, he says. The night breeze is like a tonic for the kite. Kites love night-time – there are no birds to disturb the peace. Kites are sensitive beings and don't like being startled.

Kumar cannot wait for nightfall. Father thinks he is a natural talent at flying kites. He wants to practise flying the kite in the night breeze, after his parents are asleep. There is a brisk zephyr blowing across the Kaveri River, which meanders through India's southern states. The rope chafes his young hands. He practises the moves to throw the kite. The kite takes off, demanding its freedom; like a caged bird, finally free. Kumar's fingers hold on to the last bit of rope. He feels sweat trickle down his spine and then cool in the night breeze. He can see the kite flying against the moonlight, like a bat. After a while, his right hand gets tired. He changes hands. This kite really wants to fly. Ever since he got the kite as a present, Kumar is more tired in the mornings. Sunlight wafts in, as he gulps down his rice porridge and walks to school. He can't wait for the night to darken. At night, no one can see him practising. He wakes one eye up first, the other squinting, still sleepy. Tonight Raman is coming with him.

They meet on the bank of the river.

Mosquitoes attack them. Mosquitoes love the legs of little boys. Raman wears chappals on his feet. The chappals have become small. His toes stick out on either side of the strap.

Kumar thinks he is mighty good. Raman is not

so sure of Kumar's ability, but does not say so. He wants to learn to fly the kite. He can't wait for school to finish each day.

The local school has all but disappeared as parents are beginning to send their children to schools in big towns like Salem. However, Salem is over two hours away by bus, and only those that have relatives in the big town can send their children there, as they have to stay there during the week. It is difficult to find a teacher willing to teach a school of only a hundred kids, which is unusual in a country of eight hundred million people. But, then, KKP is a special village. Ten thousand people live in KKP.

This is a particularly difficult year. The crops have been affected by poor rainfall, and the nearby Mettur dam lacks its usual mojo. Kumar is at school, sitting under the banyan tree. This banyan tree is huge – and has more arms than any of the goddesses in the temple. The classes are held outdoors. There are only two classes, one for primary-school pupils, and the other for high-school pupils. When it rains, they grab their pads made of black slate and pieces of chalk and run indoors to the large hut, which is the school hall. It has walls made of brick and cement, which are about three to four feet tall. From the walls, there are several bamboo poles rising up. On these poles rests a large thatched roof. It keeps the kids cool during the oppressively hot and dry summers. There has been talk of erecting a permanent roof, but people say that might mean the kids will be stuck with the same school in their next life; keeping the roof thatched and impermanent will make sure the gods will bless the kids with a big plush city school in their next life.

People say that the three seasons in Tamil Nadu are hot, hotter and the monsoon. However, this year, the monsoon failed and it is going to be a dry hot season.

Gowrie teacher says dreams belong amongst clouds; otherwise people will not have to move mountains to reach them. Raman dreams of leaving school. He wants to go to a big city – a big city like Madras. Not this shitty village where they all have to go to the water pump and fill their buckets. The Kaveri is just beside them, yet no one has water running from taps.

'Teacher Amma, do Christians believe in rebirth?'

'No Raman, not in the way that we Hindus do,' she answers. 'They believe they live once and after that depending on the good or bad they do, they go to Heaven or Hell.'

Being a Hindu sounds good to Raman. At least he gets another shot at life. Maybe he'll get lucky and be married to a film star in his next birth. Beyond the school there is a curved path which slopes down towards the river. It is a ten-minute walk. Porpoises have been known to make an appearance here, albeit rarely.

Very few people, even today, know about the Kaveri River porpoises. These look like dolphins, except they have a blunter nose and look rather like mini whales. They migrate during the rainy season, although the Mettur dam has somewhat restricted their domain. These porpoises are playful and let the kids wade near them. They swim only on their right sides, nodding their heads continually. 'Hey look! The small one is riding on the other's back!'

'Wow!'

It is said that if you see porpoises playing in the Kaveri, you can be sure that no demons or monsters are about, as the porpoises will drive them away. 'I wish I had a porpoise at home,' whispers Lakshmi. Lakshmi attends the same class and is a good friend of Kumar and Raman. Once the weather becomes warmer, the porpoises migrate towards the Kaveri delta, looking for the ocean beyond. Kumar finds a green soda bottle with a marble stopper that bobs up and down, like a valve. He thinks it might bring him luck.

Kumar and Raman walk to school with Lakshmi.

Raman is Kumar's best friend.

'Do you think your parents are unhappy?' asks Raman.

'*My* parents?' says Kumar.

'Yeah.'

'They seem OK.'

'Kadallaikaran says that only unhappy couples or couples in Communist China stop with one child. That given a choice, everyone would have more than one child.'

From that moment, Kumar feels a bit different. Until that day, he had felt special; like his parents had chosen not to have another child so that they could concentrate on his well-being. Now, suddenly, this theory questions his logic. He feels a trifle insecure. 'You think I should ask my Mum and Dad if they are happy?'

'You can't ask them things like that!'

'I guess.' Kumar still feels short-changed.

Raman has two brothers and a sister.

'Why do you think your parents had only one child?' asks Lakshmi.

'I don't know, perhaps they only wanted one child.'

'Do you wish you had brothers and sisters?' she asks.

'Come to think of it, I have never really thought about it,' Kumar confesses.

Raman interrupts. 'Lucky bastard, that way you'll inherit all the family land. I've got to share with two brothers. Well, at least it is better than Lakshmi; as a girl she gets no land at all; she just gets married off.'

'I don't want to be married off,' replies Lakshmi indignantly.

Raman laughs; whenever Raman laughs or smiles, his mouth curls up to the left side, like a hockey stick.

The night kite-flying practice sessions continue. Tonight, Lakshmi has decided to tag along. The boys don't mind. She is not like other girls. Lakshmi can be counted on to keep things quiet. Lakshmi brings burfi for them to eat. The burfi is delicious. Today, she has brought Raman's favourite, chocolate burfi.

Lakshmi says that the boys have fox-bellies. Like the story in the Mahabharata where Bhima is always hungry – it is said Bhima has a belly like a fox, not fat but hungry. Kumar recalls reading the story where Bhima crushes Bakkasura, the glutton-demon, in his arms. Food extrudes out of each of the demon's nine orifices. Kumar points out the nine orifices on his body. They laugh. Kumar is hungry for more chocolate burfi. Lakshmi's burfis *are* the best.

Tonight the moon is small. Or their eyes are big. Their eyes get used to the dark. They huddle under a blanket. The blanket is not for the cold, but to keep the mosquitoes from biting their legs. Lakshmi has made a lot of burfis. Soon there are none left. 'Tomorrow I'll make a different sweet, perhaps jalebis,' Lakshmi declares.

The boys don't argue. Cooking is girl territory.

'It is nice here, just the three of us,' Lakshmi says, with her mouth full. 'We're like three legs of a stool.'

'Whatever.'

They take turns flying the kite. When it is Lakshmi's turn they anchor the rope of the kite on a tree, so she can't lose the kite. Girls can lose things easily.

Kumar knows Lakshmi likes Raman. Kumar likes Lakshmi too, but his special feelings are reserved for Gowrie teacher. He hears the Kaveri River sigh. He breathes deeply. He sighs too. Lakshmi thinks she is doing as well as the boys. 'That is because we are all the same height,' she says.

It is true, Kumar thinks. They *are* more or less the same height.

Raman is fair-skinned, with longish dark hair. His hair is almost shoulder length.

'Your hair is so long and thick. You could pass for a girl,' Lakshmi says.

'Don't be ridiculous!'

Kumar thinks Raman is good-looking, almost pretty. Raman's face is prettier than most girls in class, he thinks. Raman's skin is unusually light for a Tamil, Kumar thinks as he surveys his own dark brown forearms.

Lakshmi turns to Kumar. 'Your hair is all curly and wobbly.'

Kumar pulls a strand of hair from his forehead and squints to inspect it. The hair springs back as soon as he lets go. They all laugh.

Lakshmi's hair is getting longer. It cascades down her back. She has wide-set brown eyes, which give her a perennial look of surprise.

'How much time do we have left?' Raman asks.

'A month, for the big competition in Salem.'

Kite-flying is big in cities like Salem and Madras – mainly among the fishermen. Perhaps they have more time to dream, and more things they can only dream about. Kumar takes out the broken glass from his pocket. It is what remains of his green soda bottle. He has it wrapped in paper, so that it does not cut his pocket. The glass has been shredded to a coarse grain. At night, the glass glistens in the moonlight like a million gemstones. Lakshmi likes the look of the glass.

'What are you going to do with it?' she asks.

'It's for the manja – the stuff that coats the kite rope.'

Raman gets out the bag of dog shit. He opens the cloth bag. The nai pee stinks. It opens their sinuses.

Lakshmi is disgusted. Kumar inspects it critically.

'It is too stodgy, we can't use the paper. We have to finish it by hand.'

Lakshmi stands a safe distance away.

Kumar painstakingly mixes the broken glass with the dog shit. He and Raman then coat the rope of the kite with the admixture. Will the dog-shit manja be enough to win the battles in Salem? Kumar thinks about all the different manja bases he has tried, from wheat flour to clay, but the dog shit holds the glass manja best. It will make their kite a lethal weapon during the duels. Raman is good at mixing the manja.

Lakshmi recites a prayer, wishing them luck. She prays to the elephant-god, Ganesha. Her mother says that one must always pray to Ganesha before any new venture. Lakshmi likes the Ganesha story. She asks her mother to tell it to her every week. Mother always embellishes the story differently, but the essence is the same. Lakshmi likes the little changes in the story.

Mother says they are not changes, just different spices in the story. A good story is like a good meal, she says. They both fill you up with satisfaction until you nearly burst; choosing the spices carefully is the essence of both.

Ganesha is the son of Lord Shiva and the Goddess Parvati. Lord Shiva is away a lot, and Parvati asks Ganesha to guard the home from strangers. When

Shiva returns, it is after so long that Ganesha does not recognise him. He refuses to let him in. A huge battle ensues. Shiva, known for his raging temper, cuts Ganesha's head off. Parvati is furious and Shiva rushes to find a replacement head to restore Ganesha's life. He needs the first animal head he comes across. So, Ganesha ends up with an elephant head. Parvati worries that Ganesha will become a source of ridicule; she prays that he will become the most important of the gods – the one people will worship first, before a new quest.

Lakshmi does not like Shiva much. He seems a bit boorish. She hopes she will never end up with a husband like Shiva. She does not tell her mother that, though.

It is almost time for the competition.

The next morning the boys will go to Salem to compete against big men and their kites. Like a couple of little elephant-gods fighting against Shivas, Lakshmi thinks. She hopes their kite does not get its head chopped off.

Kumar reckons the nai pee manja holds the key to their success. Father says all that a kite needs to fly is a gust of a dream. Kites have wings, men don't. Men need dreams to reach beyond roofs, trees and to dance amongst the clouds. Kites need men to control them, to keep their dreams sane.

Kumar rises early. He is excited. He checks the kite. Some of the dog shit has come off. 'Fuck,' he swears, like a grown man – 'FUCK!' Even his voice sounds grown up when he curses.

Kadallaikaran has arrived. He is pushing his groundnut trolley. He fries the groundnuts on charcoal. He salts them and rolls them up in cones of newspaper. He hears Kumar swear. Cursing and swearing makes one feel better, he says. It is therapeutic. Bad words need to come out just like bad wind. No point in holding back swear words, just as there isn't any point in holding back a fart.

Mother's voice sounds angry. 'What were you saying, Kumar?'

'A curse,' Kumar whispers. But his grown-up voice has disappeared. He sounds more timid and familiar, even to himself. There is something he does not understand. Cursing is bad. Everyone knows that. But for a moment, it felt good – *real* good. Father says real good is how a dog feels when it licks its bollocks. Cursing felt dog-bollocks-good.

Raman pokes his head around the door. 'Ready?'

It is good to have wings, even if on a kite. It is even better to have a second pair of hands, today. The sun is rising fast. The light is bathing the treetops, and is demarcating the rooftops. Raman has brought some onions. They peel them quickly. They put an onion under each armpit and stand under the strong sun. In a short while their armpits begin to burn. They pretend to be ill. There is only one medical clinic in the village, a small clinic where a doctor visits on Fridays. The doctor wears a white coat. It smells of sweat and liniment. The doctor's face is all crumpled. He must be old, or very sleepy, Raman thinks. His coat is far too big. Perhaps it is because the government only makes one-size doctors' coats. Loose folds of the white coat hang down the old doctor's back like wings on a stork; an ageing stork, Kumar thinks.

'What's the problem?' he asks wearily.

'Fever, sir.' From his pocket the doctor takes out a thermometer. He shakes it vigorously. He sticks the thermometer under their armpits.

'One hundred and two degrees. No school for you both,' he declares. He writes a prescription for some fever medicine. Kumar wonders how a doctor who studies for five years in a medical college can be fooled in five minutes. And that too with a lowly onion! Doctors are good with the human body, but are hopeless with the human mind, Father often says. They pack the kite carefully in a gunny bag and walk briskly towards the bus stop. Lakshmi passes them.

She wishes them luck. They tell her the story about fooling the doctor. She laughs, nodding her head. Her hair is wet. It is Friday. All good Hindu girls wash their hair on Fridays – for the Friday pooja and temple prayers. The girls in class usually wear their hair loose on Fridays, as their hair is damp. In the English movies, women dry their hair with blowing machines. Here, the sun does all the drying, and the wind does all the blowing.

Lakshmi's hair reaches down to her butt. Kumar notices her butt for the first time. It wiggles as she walks. Lakshmi is developing a wiggle. Kadallaikaran says that a girl developing a wiggle is a first sign of womanhood. He knows women – even British women. British people have it all wrong, Kadallaikaran says. The women wear their hair short, and the men wear it long. Some women in Scotland wear pants, and men wear skirts.

With a plume of dust, the bus appears. The boys bid farewell to Lakshmi.

'We'll go and come.' Everyone knows that one must never say that one is leaving or one is just going. That implies never to return, and brings bad luck. In Tamil, people always say, 'I shall go and come'.

Kumar crumples up the doctor's prescription and throws it out the bus window. He aims for the gutter, and misses. They are on their way to Salem. Raman

holds on to the gunny bag. The kite is in the gunny
bag.

At Salem, the kite competition is held in a big
playground. There is a coconut tree nearby. Kumar
motions to Raman, who begins climbing the tree. It
will be his job to call out the wind shifts.

'North wind,' he says.

A north wind is notoriously treacherous, more
unpredictable than a south wind. Kumar knows the
task at hand. It is all about harnessing the power of
the wind. The kite must ascend slowly, rung by rung
on an imaginary ladder to the gods. Many kites are
flying. They float up like a zillion dreams. Dreams
need to be released, to find a way out. Otherwise,
dreams will go mouldy inside the mind. Mouldy
dreams are no good. Mouldy minds are even worse,
says Father.

Kumar hears the traffic nearby, the cry of the
street vendors, and the noise of the crows. But his
eyes are fixed on the kite. Their kite is bright red.
Behind them many men are placing bets. This is
serious business. People want blood. They want
money. Raman and Kumar are purists. They are here
to test their skills, to hone their technique. The kites
are puppets for the punters hedging their bets. The

boys feel like puppets in the hands of grown-ups. Their kite is christened *China Moon* due to its red colour, by the men arranging the bets. Right next to them is a man flying a kite the colour of the Indian flag, the tricolour. His kite is called the *Indian Tiger*. He is standing so close that Kumar can see the veins standing up in his temples.

'South-west,' Raman calls out as the wind shifts. Kumar changes his grip and gives the kite more freedom. It bucks like a bull. It strains, trying to slice through the clouds. Kumar moves his feet apart, so that he can keep his balance. His right and left hands rise at the same time, and his kite muscles strain.

Their kite rope comes into contact with another nearby kite. The dog-shit manja is a success. Their rope cuts the rope of the other kite like a knife through soft ghee. The man standing next to Kumar has noticed that. He has razor blades stuck on his rope. Without warning, he shoves Kumar. Raman slides down the coconut tree and comes to Kumar's aid. He grabs the kite's rope, his hands getting stronger with determination. Kumar pushes the man back, his suddenness surprising the man, who moves back with a jolt. The crowd moves closer, wanting to watch the action. The backers of *China Moon* shout to the man to back off. Now there are only two kites left. It is a duel!

Raman feels strong enough to send the kite to the moon. The kite seems to be getting lighter in his hands. It won't be long now before the end game begins. They will have to decapitate the other kite. For a moment, a sense of patriotism makes Raman pause. How can he cut off the Indian flag? The wind blows against his face and soothes him. It seems to say, 'This is just a game.' The shouts of the punters ring in his ears. They are baying for blood. He manoeuvres the kite towards the Indian tricolour. The man's face is changing colour, though. It has turned red. He hurls abuse at them. Then he jams his kite onto theirs, in an attempt to cut their kite off with the razor blades. But the nai pee manja does the job. The other kite's rope is severed and the *Indian Tiger* flies away, like the man's broken dream.

'I'm sorry, sir,' Kumar tries to apologize but his voice is drowned out by the cheering crowd. People are rushing about collecting cash from their bets. *China Moon* has won. *Indian Tiger* has lost. 'Fucking China has killed India again,' a voice shouts. The voice sounds heavy, laden with the local broth. The broth is being brewed in the corner, right in the playground. The broth is a mixture of local arrack, coconut toddy and several other ingredients. Raman can see someone dumping old batteries into the broth to give it more bite. Kumar and Raman get carried

off by the crowd on their shoulders. Raman's hands
let go of *China Moon*. Someone in the crowd takes off
with it. The boys are getting scared. The crowd is
getting unruly. They struggle until they are brought
to the ground. They hastily run to the bus stop. They
turn back for a last look at *China Moon*, now in the
hands of strangers. Kumar whispers a silent prayer
for *China Moon*. He knows father will not be pleased
that he has lost the kite. Raman wonders if they must
try and retrieve their kite. But they realize that this
is a time for discretion, not valour. Timing is
everything – in life, and while flying kites.

They are bone weary and fox-bellied by the time they
reach KKP. Lakshmi waits for them at the bus stop.

'What are you doing, out this late?' they ask.

'Waiting for you both; someone found the
doctor's prescription you threw out the bus window.
The headmaster is very angry.'

Veerappan is the head of the village panchayat.
As well as being in charge of the assembly he also
functions as the headmaster of the school.

Anger has cauterized the headmaster's tongue,
and initially he does not speak. His glaring eyes do
the talking. He looks angry, his moustache reiterating
his importance. Finally he engages in a fiery diatribe,

ending with his decision. He suspends the boys from school for the rest of the year.

Kumar feels sad. He will miss Gowrie teacher. Raman is not sad. He thinks he has had enough of school anyway.

Raman thinks he might become a tailor. He is good with scissors. His cutting skills have been honed from making and testing kites. He will travel to Madras and live with his uncle who is a tailor there.

3

THE TRAIN LEAVES KKP station. Raman can't wait to reach the big city. His hopes are suspended like stars in the sky, of unknown futures. The train departs the station at night. Raman cranes his neck to wave goodbye to his parents, standing on the platform. The lone figure of Kumar stands well back from the train. Kumar's eyes seem misty. Raman knows they will miss each other.

He shouts out, 'I shall go and come!'

The train gains speed. Raman hears clamour of metal as wheels change track, muffled sounds of footfalls, murmuring of the wind in the moonlight and sounds of sleep. He sees a man sitting in the berth in front of him, devouring a bunch of grapes. Every now and then Raman spies a gold tooth as the man bends over to spit the grape skins under the seat. The grape skins have formed a small hillock. The train is now on a long bridge across the Kaveri River. Raman remembers when Kumar and he used to place five-paisa coins on the tracks for the train to run over.

People say that the coins will turn into little magnets.
It never happens to their coins, though. They simply
get flattened out of shape. Their coins have never
been lucky.

Raman notices the red paint on the outside of
the train flaking as he leans over to catch a glimpse
of the water. He hears the rumble of thunder. The
sky parts like a curtain and a few drops of rain fall
like sweat onto his outstretched palm. He feels the
coolness against his skin. His heart begins to beat
faster.

The man opposite him watches him impassively,
still spitting out grape skins. 'What caste are you?'
he asks gruffly.

'Gounder,' Raman whispers.

In Tamil Nadu, everyone is 'something' – Hindu,
Christian, Muslim, Gounder, Chettiar, Mudaliar or
Brahmin. One cannot be an ordinary human being
here. The first question a stranger asks a fellow Tamil
is 'What are you?'

A passenger announces that the ticket collector
has been sighted in the next compartment and will
be along shortly to check the tickets. Having finished
with spitting out grape skins, which are piled up like
a peak of the Shevaroy Hills, the man begins to roll
up tobacco into a beedi. He puts the beedi in his
mouth and gently chews on it. Raman can see the

tobacco smoke wafting out of his nostrils. Raman turns away to avoid the stench of the beedi. He can see the outline of the Shevaroy Hills, standing majestically in the distance. Raman studies his ticket. He cannot believe it. He is going to Madras! He knows he cannot hide the excitement from his face. He wipes the rainwater off his hands. The train carriage has rows and rows of bunk-like sleeping berths which are being readied for the night. People are standing up, in the hesitant incandescence of the naked electric bulbs, and spreading out their bedsheets.

Seeing the grape skins under the seat makes Raman think about his school. Gowrie teacher used to say that the Tamil language makes sense, unlike English. Why would a language have different names for dried grapes and fresh grapes? In Tamil, they are all *draksha*. In English the dried ones are called raisins or sultanas, she says.

The night darkens. Raman sees the sky dim, and the stars brighten like frost on the dark hair of the sky. His shoulders feel chilly through his wrinkled shirt. The train cabin is now filled with stale odours – old shoes, snoring breath and, of course, grape skins.

The wind starts huffing and puffing harder on the window panes, trying to keep pace with the train engine. Raman can see a few little mosquitoes lined along the edges of the glass. Every now and then he sees drunks or stray dogs relieve themselves beside the tracks.

The train smells of stale beedis. Every few seconds the carriage is filled with the monotonous double-clang of wheels on the tracks. The train continues towards Madras, the headlights illuminating the darkness, looking ahead towards his dream. The south is now at the train's back; the south with his roots, his disappointment; the north lies ahead, resplendent with his hopes.

The train stops at several towns. Most of the railway stations look the same, though. The doors open and he can identify the creaking of the hinges. He hears bustling voices boarding the train, and sees porters bringing in luggage with the expressions of men who have to do the same job over and over.

He sees ticket collectors on the platforms. He falls asleep, in the most liberal sense. He resists sleep with all his might and, at last, he decides to lean back and dream a moment so that he will wake up refreshed. He stretches out in the limited space of his berth and tries to dream. He doesn't have to try very hard. During the night he has a dream. He dreams of being chased by a monster. The monster has white hair and long limbs and a trunk like an elephant. The trunk

40

is short – sort of an elephant trunk chopped in half. Raman runs hard. He is breathing faster. He reaches the Kaveri. He is shaking, not with the night breeze but with the warmth of the Kaveri River in his veins. There is a large porpoise swimming backwards. Sure enough, when the monster sees the porpoise, he disappears. Sometimes he opens his eyes and it feels like the train has stopped moving. He sees unseen people delivering unheard words, muffled by the carriage's misty glass windows, on platforms of unknown stations.

Raman wakes early. The early rays of the sun have appeared. This train is cunning. It knows to change its shadows and trick the earth. When the smoke from its engine becomes too much, it steals some freshness from the river breeze. The smoke drifts northwards, its plume ruffled. It preens and squabbles for space with the river breeze. It then gathers momentum, as a single cloud of blackish smoke, following an imperceptible volition. In the end it blows over the plains and Raman can see the sea in the distance. Raman spies bougainvillea along an unfinished wall. They are passing another village. The bougainvillea is bright but the village is not. Not like Madras, he thinks. Soon the train passes more villages and Raman looks at the greenness of the plains. How green the grass is! Soon he spies the surface of the sea. It looks shy, like a desert, but beckons him into its grey cloak. He is in Madras!

The houses and trees seem to be zigzagging all over the place. This is a disorderly world, although Raman is sure it has all been done with a plan in mind.

The train stops at the station; people get off hurriedly, with no fuss. Luggage porters charge into the carriages looking for their next meal and pack of cigarettes. Even at that early hour, the Madras Central Station is crowded.

Raman sees many people waiting to greet their relatives and friends. The long benches are full. Some children are restless and running around the platform, playing. Mothers are carrying infants in their arms. Porters rush on ahead, carrying suitcases on turbans on their heads. Some of the faces he sees are serious and preoccupied with the business of travel; others smile in anticipation of many reunions.

Raman sees a few women dressed in garish saris. Their faces are a bit manly and they keep looking into different carriages. They all have thick black hair and deepish voices. As they approach, Raman hears one laugh – a laugh that rises above the others and curdles his blood.

'Fucking *alis*,' he hears a porter curse.

'Don't let those damn eunuchs hear you. Or

they'll cast a spell and make you impotent,' replies another porter.

Raman also sees men carrying their luggage towards the car parks. In a few hours he will be at his uncle's home. Instead of waiting on the platform like he is supposed to, he decides to walk closer to the main doorway so that he can see his uncle approaching.

Raman does not remember what happens next. He remembers hands closing on his throat from behind. '*Ayyo! Ayyo!*' he tries to scream but he is unable to form any words.

He remembers later how his eyes bulged outwards from pressure in his head. He tries to fight and hears shouting. Then he slumps down as a strong arm grabs him and he feels a heavy stick on his head. He is unconscious for some time.

When he comes to, he is in a car. There are two or three people with him. They are wearing saris, but their armpits stink like men. The alis at the train station, he thinks. Raman feels sick, the movement of the car worsening his unease. The sickness rises in his gullet as he tries to throw himself towards a door. He feels a searing on his skin as one of the alis grabs his forearm and long nails rake his flesh. He struggles and thrashes. His mind screams out a sharp angry warning. Then he hears another warning; this time, it is the leader of the pack. 'Shut up! Or we'll kill you!'

Raman is beyond reason. He is a kite flyer. A kite always wants to escape.

Kumar and he have tried to tame kites, but they are blind irrational paper beasts. He will never stay with a band of eunuchs. They will never be able to tame him!

The next time he comes to, he thinks he might be dead. This might be the netherworld. The room is pitch black and everything is silent, except for a dark eerie sound. The pain is unbearable. Can one feel pain when one is dead? he wonders. The hurt rises from his groin, through his private parts; his testicles throb, and he smells blood. He tries to sit up, but realizes he is restrained. He is blindfolded but manages to push the blindfold to one side. He feels a surge of relief that he can see. Raman looks down. There is blood everywhere! He feels fear erupt inside him and he tries to control it as he frees one hand from the binding and reaches for his genitals. Then he sees blood and pus on his hands. There is nothing to feel but a raw wound. He can feel the bile rising in his throat. He passes out. Then the nightmare begins.

Raman cannot remember how many days have passed. He loses all appetite, and at night shakes with fever. He tries to get up, but his brain feels fuzzy and he lies down again Alien noises seep through the walls, and his brain tries to interpret them. As evening comes around, the grilles on the windows grow blurred. A chilly shade seems to spring out of the walls. Raman is numb. He is not sure if he can feel the cold. At nights he keeps repeating, 'Escape! Escape!' He keeps repeating this refrain as day breaks. In the distance, a cock crows, interrupting his words. He realizes the naivety of his thoughts, and tears pour down his face. Raman hears muffled footsteps as the eunuchs come by his door. He closes his eyes to a thin slit and pretends to be asleep.

A rough hand against his face makes him jump. He sees the leader of the eunuchs looking at him. Her teeth are misshapen and stained red from chewing betel leaves. He names this one The Evil One.

The Evil One smiles. 'You didn't have to struggle so much.'

'Where am I?'

'In our harem – where we alis live.'

'When can I go home?'

'This is your home now. We are your family.' The Evil One's calm, matter-of-fact tone angers him further. 'Let me take a look at the wound,' says The Evil One.

Raman struggles. He screams. Screams rise from him like the howls of a wolf talking to its spirits. He feels the hairs rise on the back of his neck. He feels hands anointing him with turmeric and saffron. He is powerless to resist. His world has changed. The screaming inside him stops, in surrender.

The Evil One is saying something to the others. Raman tries to hear, but his ears feel as though they have been plugged with cotton wool. He hears something about making him a proper lady.

Then, without warning, The Evil One kicks him in the groin, reopening the healing wound. The wound already filled with pus and a forming cicatrix reopens, with the smell of death. Raman passes out again, his mouth still open, in a silent scream.

'When the hole now heals, you will be a proper woman,' says The Evil One.

He finds a dusty window. He clears away some dust with the back of his sweaty hand and peers outside, like a ghost. He sees alis coming to the house, through the window. They are carrying a lamp, singing a litany and applying turmeric paste on their bodies. They are carrying out a ritual he does not understand. He understands nothing. He feels a mist hovering around his eyes and everything seems hazy. One of the eunuchs burns some camphor; the smell drifts across the room, mingling with the smell of blood.

He sees his reflection in the window. In the clothes he has been adorned with, he looks like a girl. His lips touch the glass of the window, his breath now forming mist on the glass. The eunuchs are behind him and lighted candles have been placed, at his feet. He can hear litanies being sung, faintly. The litany rises to a loud crescendo. The eunuchs begin to accompany it, through strained, joyous voices. Raman looks at them. Their saris are white today. He can make out the outline of The Evil One behind him, although he is still too scared to turn around. The Evil One lifts him up, scooping him up.

'I christen you Ramani, adopted daughter of the Lord Ganesha, your protector. Accept therefore this chain of faith as a sign from Lord Ganesha. From now on you will be called Ramani.'

Ramani does not know exactly what happened, but time changes after that moment. It is as if resistance has slipped out of her weakened grasp. Days pass. Nights pass. She is no longer restrained. In any case, she is too weak to run away. The smell of blood and pus lingers in her head. It is still on her after she bathes. She can taste it on her lips and cannot sleep at night. She feels horror and disgust. Something else, a different fear grips her – a fear of a path she has never seen before. She does not know if she is going forwards or back or merely out of her mind. She falls into a sleep. In her sleep, Mother comes to her and touches her. She sees blood on her hands, and screams. Then she sees the murdered bodies of eunuchs littering the room. She sees two bodies on her right and two on her left. The bodies all have a slash across their throats, to match the slash in their groins. Then Mother is gone. She shouts. She feels cold. The cold goes deeper and deeper into her bones.

Her room has no lock or handle. At times, through a window which opens into a corridor, she can see the silhouette of one of the alis. She realizes there are three of them. The leader is the garish one with the bad teeth, who is called Rajinder; the one she has named The Evil One. The second one wears glasses and seems studious, like a librarian. She names her The Professor; her name is Kamalam. The third is pretty. She is fair and petite, with dimpled cheeks. She wears her sari very low and stands with her legs apart. Kadallaikaran used to say prostitutes stand like that. As a groundnut seller, he gets to see everyone. The pimp and the prostitute both eat peanuts, he used to say. Ramani names the third ali The Hooker.

Ramani misses Kadallaikaran, the village and her friends, especially Kumar and Lakshmi. Ramani even misses going to school. This transition from the land of dreams to the land of nightmares has been rapid. She is being held by lunatics.

Sunlight falls in squares through the grilles on the windows. The Hooker pushes the window open. 'Can you see it?' she asks.

'What?' She does not even want to talk to her.

'The sea. I love the sea. It is always in my head. I think it is the sea which keeps me from going to sleep at night, with its whispers. Have you ever seen the sea?'

Ramani shakes her head. 'I've spent a lot of time in the Kaveri River,' she says.

They hear sporadic sounds from the seashore close by. There is a wet slapping sound as the sea nuzzles against the rocks. The seashore is full of people. The sea seems monstrously huge, with no beginning or end.

'Marina Beach is better. Has lots of sand. Here there are mainly rocks. Marina Beach is the second-longest beach in the world,' says The Hooker proudly, with the enthusiasm of a tour guide.

'Come with me, let's walk on the seashore,' she says.

Ramani struggles to her feet, still groggy. She feels

a dull pain between her legs. She walks out of the house with The Hooker. She can see the watchful eyes of The Evil One behind them. She feels the cool wind blowing from the sea. It is different from the river breeze. It is salty and smells. At first the smell stifles her; there seems to be too many odours to take in. She longs for the rich soil, blossoming trees and rounded rocks of the river bank. Instead, she sees sand, seashells and mildly undulating dunes. She sees some fish, dead and half eaten by the seagulls. Even the dead fish are different here. They are dried out by the sun, their eye sockets empty and their half-eaten bodies filled with sand.

Ramani looks across at The Hooker. She seems a bit different on the seashore. She is still pale and a bit thin, but some fire has crept into her beautiful face. The sea seems to have restored her energy. Ramani feels a bit renewed too, by the salty sea air. The sea seems to be a living animal, but its life seems different to that of the river. The river lives more like an antelope, bounding and leaping and nibbling at the grass. The sea is more human, seems to breathe in and breathe out. The tide moves in and out, irrespective of the kind of day it is. The sea cuts us off from the rest of the world, our enemies and distant lands. The river is different, constantly seeking to build bridges and live as a part of the village. The river belongs to the village. The sea has its own family; people here say the sea has two brothers: the moon and the wind. The sea cannot live without them. The moon sucks up the life of the sea and causes high tide, while the wind tosses the sea's hair, making it stir and rustle in all directions.

Ramani looks down at the water constantly rising and falling on the sand. She sees flat, pinkish, plastic-like creatures, shaped like hands, rushing along the beach. They have five fingers and two pincers out of the head. They contract when startled, but run across the sand with nightmare speed.

Ramani is fascinated.

'Sand crabs – the famous Madras mud crabs,' The Hooker informs her.

'River crabs are much smaller and more rounded,' answers Ramani.

They see children chase them and women flee at the approach of these spidery crabs.

'Grab one,' urges The Hooker.

'I can't,' says Ramani, momentarily forgetting her pain.

This moment with the crabs amuses her. She no longer feels the concrete, savage and immovable terror that had gripped her earlier. It is a veritable declaration of truce, a freedom within a prison to be alive. She even feels a brief twinge of sisterhood with The Hooker.

The Hooker digs a hole. 'Grab a few crabs and put them at the bottom,' she says. She picks up four crabs and tosses them quickly into the hole, carefully avoiding the pincers.

As Ramani looks down into the pit, she sees the crabs trying to reach the top. At first the crabs seem to be helping each other, by standing on each other so that one can reach the top. But every time a crab reaches the top, after great effort, it is pulled down by one of the others. One of the crabs, the big one, seems rash enough to try and reach the top quickly, without help. But when this crab is about to topple over the top one of the others pulls him down.

'You would think that one of the crabs would reach the top, but it doesn't seem to happen,' says Ramani.

'Of course not,' says The Hooker. 'You throw crabs in a pit and they are stuck there. Within a few minutes of being in a hole together, the need to prevent someone else getting ahead creeps into their veins. Rajinder says that is human nature.'

She feels a raging resentment towards The Hooker. She is ashamed that this vexation seems close to affection. This playing on the beach has brought them into sisterly contact, with anger, friendliness and hatred causing great turmoil in her mind.

Ramani does not think of it at that time, but later

she thinks about the mud crabs in the pit. They move unsteadily – like a walking three-legged stool, she thinks. Lakshmi used to say Kumar, Raman and she were like the three legs of a stool. Take a leg off, and the equilibrium is disturbed. Lakshmi used to use that line to make sure she was included in the night kite-flying sessions.

Ramani longs for her village, and her friends. I am stuck, she thinks – stuck like a mud crab in a sand pit. She looks up to the sky at Lord Ganesha, and wonders if he is feeling her pain. He must, she reasons. After all, his head was cut off. She tries to smile through her tears, at the inadvertent pun. If he could make a success of his abominable cut, she must. At least she does not have an elephant trunk on her neck. That image makes her smile. Lord Ganesha seems to tell her to not stand bowed down as if an elephant head is on her shoulders. Stand tall, Ramani, he says, and be proud of your courage.

Lord Ganesha's life story gives her strength. She can resign herself to life in this garb, and a new identity, she reasons; but not for a life with these kidnappers. If escape becomes a possibility, I have to do it quietly, alone and trusting no one, she thinks.

4

KUMAR IS TESTING kites. He has three kites to test. He takes the first one, which is tubular and made of plastic. Kumar has made it out of a large plastic carton he found. Kumar is by himself, testing the flight patterns of the kites. He is calm, his expression blank and closed; content. Kites allow his thoughts to escape with them.

The plastic kite is too heavy. Or the wind is too light. It gets trapped in the bushes on the crest of the slope on the river bank.

He slides down on all fours vigorously to retrieve the kite. He sees a shadow ahead, breathing hard.

Kadallaikaran? He is standing by a *Kumudam* magazine. The popular gossip magazine is opened at a page which reveals a photo of an actress in a bikini. Kadallaikaran has his *sunni*, his kipper, out and is pulling it vigorously. Kumar coughs nervously to attract his attention.

'Oh! You,' Kadallaikaran says. 'Cut out the surprised look. Don't you ever jerk off?' he asks.

Kumar is not sure what he means, so he tells him that.

Kadallaikaran squeezes his sunni and moves it around till it is hard.

'It's thick,' Kumar says, as Kadallaikaran spits on his palms and rubs the saliva in. Then he starts pulling his kipper again. Kumar is shocked by his familiarity, but he does not say anything. Kadallaikaran shows him the spot where you squeeze it, where the head turns violet, and how you pull it until a sticky sap oozes out.

Kumar tries it and jumps in surprise as the sticky sap oozes out of him. He bends because he has a funny tingling in his lower tummy when the sap comes out. He can't stand up straight.

Kadalliakaran says men need to jerk off – jerking off clears a man's head of sticky thoughts. The sap is what makes babies, he says. The husband and wife both make sap, he says.

The next morning, Kumar gets up earlier than usual. The sun rises early in KKP. It floods the roofs and spills onto the muddy ugliness of the village. The houses are barren, with thatched roofs, and have doors so low that one has to stoop to enter. As courtyards are often packed down with cow dung, there is the smell of cow dung everywhere. Laughter and anger are often heard at the water pump, where people congregate to fill their buckets. Laughter seems out of place in such a dry, lifeless village; almost an act against nature.

The wind from the Kaveri gets blustery. The handpump is working ceaselessly. Many arms take turns at pumping water from its spout, yet not a single arm can control it. It is like an unruly donkey. People turn it two hundred times, three hundred times, but cannot break its spirit.

Lakshmi watches the pump spellbound. All year round, villagers meet at the water pump. Love and peace and happiness and disputes are all offerings to the holy ground around it. Someone is always hand-pumping water, and then their thirst spouts wings. And just as the parched land soaks up any spilled water, all disputes begin and end at the water pump.

Kumar wants to meet Lakshmi alone in the evening. He has never met her in the evening without Raman. Now Raman is in Madras. Lakshmi whispers that she will come to the river bank with some burfis that evening. Kumar can't wait.

That evening he does not feel fox-bellied or sleepy. Something moves in his stomach, like a butterfly. It must be a butterfly. He thinks the butterfly might want to come out and see the light. Stomachs must have scary dark, coiled walls and strange smells. People here say a butterfly will fall asleep if you tell a colourful story. He tells the butterfly the story of winning the kite competition in Salem with Raman. He misses Raman. He wonders if Raman will mind him meeting Lakshmi in the evening. From the darkness of the river bank, Lakshmi emerges. Her smile widens her face from ear to ear. She sees Kumar waiting for her, flying a kite.

'Hey, kite flyer,' she greets him.

Kumar doesn't know how to answer her. The kite whistles in the wind. Lakshmi places her head near his, and they both hear the sound of the wind being sliced by the rope. She holds the rope with her fingers. Her fingers touch his. Kumar gulps. Later, they sit down on the grass. Lakshmi always has her eyes on the ground. She used to look at him before, but nowadays does not look him in the face. Kumar takes hold of her chin and pulls her face up. She closes her eyes and he gently peels them open. She looks into his eyes. Her pupils seem large. Fireflies flit out from a nearby bush. They dive elegantly back under the leaves. The leaves look like they are electric leaves. The leaves must have transmitted the electricity to them, because when they touch each other, Kumar is surprised by a jolt. Is it electricity? He is used to the jolt of a kite. Lakshmi makes a frown, crinkling up her nose as if to say she doesn't understand what happened.

The evening wind makes noise like the strings of a veena.

'*Maasil veenaiyum, maalai mathiamum*' ('The wind sings like a veena in the evening moonlight'), Lakshmi sings softly. They both sit on a blanket on the ground. The wind picks up speed, discovers their hiding place and curls up their blanket to bring them closer. It is as if until that moment the wind had not noticed that there were two of them.

The wind quietens down. The world seems to be not going anywhere. They both huddle close as it gets chilly. The Kaveri River seems to slow down, too. Lakshmi gets out the burfis. Soon their mouths and cheeks are messy.

'Dad comes home at seven. I had better be going,' Lakshmi says. She touches his messy cheek with hers. Her skin is against his and it warms him. He trembles as he feels her clothes against his, the warmth of her knee against his. She holds out a forefinger, with some burfi stuck on it. 'Want some?'

He leans over and sucks her forefinger. The burfi tastes honeyed. He holds the kite between his knees to prevent it flying away. It feels warm, too. His chest

58

seems to thud against the kite. Beneath his hard ribcage, he seems to have a molten fire. Then the fireflies switch off their lights, and it is time to go home.

Kumar tells Kadallaikaran he thinks he is in love. 'Am I too young to fall in love?' he asks the groundnut man.

'What rubbish! When does a kid learn to say *kannan* or *mazhai* properly? Just as kids learn to say *na* and *zha* words properly at different ages, love has no age. I knew it when I saw you look at Lakshmi's hips move. Don't worry, your secret is safe,' he smiles.

It must be obvious, Kumar thinks. He is going around town singing movie songs. His voice sounds strange to him these days. Strange because it has cracked and sounds hoarse. Kadallaikaran says falling in love is like catching undersize fish. Catching fish in the Kaveri is fun. But if you hold on to the undersized fish, it is no good for the years ahead. Holding on to undersize fish reduces fish populations and food. People must let the undersize fish go, he says; like love. If the fish grows and lands in your net again, that is fate. If not, it was never in your stars. Kumar feels a bit confused, but he does not say so. He helps Kadallaikaran cut newspapers into squares. He then rolls up freshly roasted peanuts in cones made of yesterday's newspaper. Kadallaikaran holds up a page. Yesterday's newspaper stories have to move forward even if they have no destination. Their letters dance and change the meaning of words. Dreams become nightmares and nightmares become dreams. One must not walk in front of yesterday, or it will feel stifled, he says. Yesterday needs to blossom into tomorrow. One cannot hide behind yesterday. One must always walk beside yesterday. Yesterday is our companion, he says. It picks you up if you fall down. Tomorrow is different. It is nosy, a nuisance. It constantly asks questions. When you dream today, it is your mind trying to answer tomorrow's nosy questions, he says.

Kumar has eaten his cone of groundnuts. He unfurls the newspaper. 'There is a lot of anti-Hindi anger in Madras,' he says.

'It is natural,' Kadallaikaran says. He shows Kumar his hands. 'My right hand is fast and tosses groundnuts easily. It understands my thoughts and responds. It is my livelihood. It is Tamil. My left hand is scatterbrained and uncoordinated. It is good only to wash my arsehole. It is Hindi,' he says.

It is the Dravidian way to unite against the enemy. The Mughals never conquered Tamil Nadu, the seat of Dravidian culture. The DMK Party (*Dravida*

Munnetra Kazhagam or Society for Advancement of Dravidians) was founded by Annadurai in 1949. He felt that outsiders could not be trusted with the welfare of the Tamils. After Annadurai died, MGR left the party, unhappy with its direction. MGR named his party after Annadurai, who was simply called Anna by his followers. That led to the formation of the Anna DMK (ADMK) Party.

In India, when a politician leaves a party he starts a new one with the same name, and adds someone's initials. Thus years later, Indira Gandhi would form her own faction of the Congress Party, the Congress-I.

'Now that Anna is no more, the ADMK is led by MGR,' Kadallaikaran says.

'Who heads the original DMK?' Kumar asks.

'Karunanidhi, MGR's eternal foe.'

'Hey, how come you know about lots of stuff, without going to university?'

Kadallaikaran points to his stack of old newspapers and magazines. 'My library,' he says.

Kumar makes another kite. This time he uses old newspapers from Kadallaikaran's trolley. His hands get smudged with the newsprint ink. He thinks he is beginning to smell like a dried inkpot. As the kite begins to fly, he can see news published in the past weeks. He remembers Kadallaikaran saying yesterday is a friend. As yesterday's news flies away before his eyes, he wonders if the kite will bring back today's dreams.

Kumar asks Kadallaikaran about marriage. When two people live together, it is like having a shave in a barber shop. In the beginning it feels nice and cosy as the lather is spread on. But the barber always brings the knife down to your throat. The knife may nick your throat or ride smoothly over your Adam's apple. Marriage is like shaving, Kadallaikaran says. You might cut yourself or get a rash but you go back for more each day. You can't avoid shaving. And the barber can't avoid the bumpiness of your Adam's apple. Love will buy you loyalty, not fidelity. It is society that buys you fidelity. That is why arranged marriages work, he says.

Kumar's mother comes out the front door. 'Kumar, stop standing in the sun, gossiping. Your face will get dark and we won't get much dowry for you,' she says.

'All right, Amma. I am coming.'

Amma smiles a lot. Her skin always looks slightly jaundiced from the turmeric paste she uses. She mixes the turmeric in buffalo milk and applies it to her face. Kumar is not allowed to say she uses buffalo milk on her face. Appa brings fresh cow's milk so that she can mix her turmeric, he tells Kadallaikaran.

'Amma, did you fall in love with Appa *before* you married him?'

'You are watching too many movies. Falling in love is for the cinema, a fantasy. I had barely met your father when I married him. Our parents had arranged the marriage.'

Kumar and Lakshmi meet on the banks of the Kaveri for the second time. They sit next to each other and watch the evening sky. The orange sun seems to drop suddenly like a giant ball thrown into the Kaveri. People say that they will never see a sun like that in a hundred years. The banyan trees' aerial roots shine yellow in the glow of the sun. The air smells of river water. The Kaveri is bumpy today. It looks like it is trying to toss out the sun from its surface. Lakshmi is deep in thought. She is wearing a red half-sari with a blue skirt. The ground is littered with fallen leaves.

'What are you thinking about?' Kumar asks.

'Love,' she says. She holds the kite and writes 'LOVE' in red letters across the newsprint.

Kumar looks at her writing on his kite. 'Kadallaikaran says falling in love is like shaving an undersize fish.'

'Shaving an undersize fish? What nonsense!' she laughs.

He lets Lakshmi release the kite. The kite rushes out of her hand. It quickly ascends towards the evening moon.

'Let me help you,' he says. He holds his hands on top of hers and moves the kite where he wants to move it. She closes her eyelids and moves with the kite, still balanced and beautiful. She follows the rhythm of the kite. Kumar feels a tingle in his little kipper. He tries to stay balanced, but he finds it difficult. His little kipper is getting agitated, sending out caresses to his raw nerves. He tries to distract himself. He listens for the movement of his fingers and looks for the final rays of sunset. He feels sweat on his back and his temples throb. The way he looks at her now is different. There is a silence in his gaze and heat in his desire. Accidentally, her hands brush against his hardness. Girls can surprise you like that.

'What was that about the undersize fish?' she laughs. Kumar's little kipper softens, its ego wounded. She asks him if she must move her hand. He stays silent, and his kipper gets restless again, against her hand; only not so undersized now.

He holds her close and is kissing her neck. His hands stray down to her breasts. His hands are trapped between their bodies at an uncomfortable angle, but he lets them rest a while on her breasts.

Kadallaikaran is right. Girls here have firm

breasts like parrot-beak mangoes.

It is the first time he has touched her and that they have held each other close. Kumar asks her if they must make love.

'We are already making love, are we not?' she says.

'I mean like married people, where we are naked and produce sap.'

No sooner has he said this than he feels ashamed at his lack of respect for her. No, Lakshmi, let us not do things old people do. We should make love, but the time is not right, he thinks.

She kisses him. No goodnight or goodbye is said that night; just a kiss, on the corner of his mouth. As she walks home, the river breeze rains kisses on her.

As Lakshmi reaches home, the light is on in the front room. She realizes that her father is home that night. Today, Mother and Father are waiting for her. When grown-ups wait together, it usually means trouble. She wishes she had a porpoise at home.

The silence and dimness of the room, the heavy eyebrows of her mother and father, make her feel uneasy. Heavy eyebrows are the beginning of bad feelings, people say.

Her parents inform her that as she has now come of age, it is time for her to be married. And, like all Gounder girls, she is to be engaged to her uncle,

Periyasamy. It is usual for girls here to marry their mother's brother.

'Mother, I don't want to marry your brother!'

'Hush, girl. You have already had your periods for three months. It is time for you to fulfil your duties as a good Gounder girl.'

Lakshmi does not like Periyasamy. I've had it with him, she thinks. She's tired of him calling her a goddess, and making her put on a lot of jewellery. In the beginning, she thought it was fun. Then he began touching her and asking her to touch him. He always tries to grope her breasts.

She tries to make her mother change her mind. She pleads with her father. She can see she is making no change to the plans in their minds. She can't even think of marrying him. She doesn't know how to tell them what he does to her. So she says nothing.

Her soul feels numb and dead. She is looking forward to seeing Kumar tomorrow, but thinks of the uselessness of it all. She is going to be married to Periyasamy the pervert, and will have to bear his child. She thinks of running away, but does not know a single place where she can go. And Kumar, how will he take it all? He will be angry, but he will not be able to do anything to stop this. She will have to be civil and polite when they meet in the future, but she is going to be married to an *asura*, a demon. This union is not meant to be, she thinks. She feels her heart beating. She sleeps fitfully, her dreams ragged. She feels restless, and her tortured heart desperately seeks an escape. She opens the window in her room. She sees spider webs and dust in the corners. She lifts a leg onto the windowsill to haul herself onto the window. She hits her elbow, and the pain makes her double over. She looks out into the darkness. The north wind is strong that night. You must get away, it tells her. Come away with me. The north wind is a notoriously treacherous wind. People here always say, never trust the north wind. She is gripped with a terrible uncertainty. Uncertainty in the knowledge that just as there is no going forward, there is no going back.

She is on the river bank. The Kaveri is a bit choppy that night. Stop pretending you are an ocean, she teases. You are just a river. The river licks at the rocks she is sitting on, trying to grab her playfully. She looks up at the moonlight and sees wispy night clouds. She takes off her chappals and steps off the rock. She hears a rustling of paper. She looks down and sees Kumar's kite – the one he made of Kadallaikaran's newspapers. He must have forgotten to take it home. She sees 'LOVE' written in red letters across its face. She feels in the fold of her half-sari. She finds her pen, with red ink. She always carries a pen with red ink. For a few minutes she sits watching the river and twisting the fountain pen in her hand. She picks up the pen and thinks of writing a note. The kite rests on her thigh. She thinks of Kumar's knee where the kite had rested. She lets her mind flood with images of him; images of him flying his kites. He had stopped short of being naked with her. He had preserved her. That feeling of his respect gives her an air of inviolacy, a privilege. She looks at her writing on the kite. She adds an 'I' and a 'YOU' to the message on the kite. It now says 'I LOVE YOU' in bright red letters. Kumar will see this, she thinks.

Suddenly the north wind gusts, picking up the kite. She stretches out to try and reach the kite. The north wind is playing games with her. It blows hard towards the river, taking her with it. She feels tears on her cheeks.

She feels river water soak her skirt, her petticoat and then work its way up her blouse. She finds her strength of breathing diminishing. She gives way to the north wind and finds some relief. She looks up at the kite, still fluttering in the wind above the Kaveri. She has let herself fall into the river. Let me drift on, she says. She feels she does not have the strength to resist. She has made her choice. First, she sees her reflection. Then, there is no reflection; just an incoherence.

Her eyes close. She can still hear the river flowing, even with water in her ears. She feels a rhythm to the beat of the river. The Kaveri is playing a song – a *ragam* of longing for love, and a *talam* of disappointment in life. She will no longer have to worry. She will have all the time she needs to make up her mind. Nothing will be forced upon her any more. The water lies cool against her face, sobering her completely. Her strength ebbs away from her, her voice and her heart.

It is now morning.

'Lakshmi is missing,' Mother wails.

'Nonsense,' says Father. He touches her pillow. It is cold to touch. He puts his hand to his chest, under his shirt. He feels an icy chill. He knows Lakshmi is like him. Nothing would make her do something she did not want to. What was he thinking? He feels like throwing up. She's gone, he thinks. My little girl is gone.

Moments later, a storm is upon them. Is it an early monsoon? It tears down roofs and destroys fences, alters the river bank and washes away paths. Heavy gusts of wind pick up the kite Kumar had left on the river bank and hurl it to a great height beneath the glowering, angry sky. The waters of the Kaveri slap and fall against the rocks. The storm lasts five days. For five days people are confined indoors. This is not a monsoon, they say. A monsoon lasts months. The Kaveri is mourning, people say.

Five days is the usual period of mourning here, after which people visit the crematorium of a dead relative. They usually pour milk on the pyre to pacify the soul. After five days the storm stops, its fury pacified. The Kaveri River has absorbed all her tears.

5

THE TWO FAT SISTERS unwrap a box covered in shiny golden paper. Inside are mittais: an assortment of sweets. There are milk khoas, cashew burfis, big round laddus and almond halwas.

The older fat sister removes the wrapper and throws it carelessly onto the road. She looks into the box, surveying the familiar contents. Two fat fingers enter the box. Then she begins to eat the sweets one by one. She eats placidly, desire and habit suffocating her self-control. The younger fat girl joins her sister in greedily devouring the packet of sweets. She has half opened her mouth to put another burfi in, when she bursts into a tumultuous shout.

'Eunuchs! *Hijras! Hijras!*' she screams, running inside.

The rest of the fat family looks at her. The fat wife makes a sign towards her husband.

The husband, no less corpulent, shrugs his shoulders as if to say, 'Let them in. I have been expecting them.'

The four eunuchs head down the street. The Professor walks with Ramani. The Evil One and The Hooker walk ahead.

'What does hijra mean?' Ramani asks.

'Hijra comes from Arabic and originally means the great migration. The great Prophet Mohammed was said to have made his hijra from Mecca to Medina. People like us, we have migrated to a third gender – not man, not woman, but a special gender; in the north of India, we are hijras, and in the south, alis,' answers The Professor.

'During the Mughal period, Emperor Akbar and the other rulers used hijras to guard their harems. They felt it would eliminate the risk of dalliances between their many wives and the guards. However, Emperor Jahangir came across one of his wives (formerly of his harem, but now no longer one of his favourites) kissing a eunuch who guarded the palace. The story goes that the Emperor Jahangir then gave the command that a round hole be made in the earth, and that his offending wife's body be put in that hole. She was made to stand with only her head above the ground. She had to stand in the parching sun until the extreme heat on her head killed her; it must have taken a few days. While a day and a night passed, and she cried out in pain, the eunuch, by the command of the Emperor, was brought out and was cut to pieces in front of her dying eyes.

'In the last century in Italy, eunuchs used to sing in the great opera performances, as they could reach high notes not reached by the male voices. The Italians called those singers "castratos". Here people do not dwell on the action that made us this way; they recognize that the migration to the third gender is necessary for the good of society. That is why the North Indians don't call us "castratos"; they call us "migratos" or hijras, instead.'

'These people are North Indians? There were no North Indians in my village,' says Ramani.

'Big cities have a lot of people from the north. They have a lot of money. The Sindhis, like these folk here, are famous for making sweets. Can't you tell by looking at their shapes? We call this family the laddu family. They are rotund and juicy, like sweet laddus.'

Ramani can't help smiling. 'What are we doing here?'

'There has been a child born to this family. Eunuchs hear about new births and weddings – through the banyan trees' hanging roots, so to speak. We are here to bless the child. If they don't want us, they'll pay us off. In general, Sindhis are very superstitious. They will do anything to ward off bad luck.'

The four eunuchs step into the house. Ramani looks around. No one looks specifically at her. She feels herself drowned in the scorn for eunuchs; first sacrificed, and now scorned by society, she thinks. These people don't even think I am different, she thinks. She does not want to be considered a eunuch. She tries to make an effort to look different; makes ugly faces, puckered faces, and a few tears trickle down her cheeks. She tries to control her tears, but two drops roll down like rivulets and rebound off her chin. She sees a little baby, being held by the mother. The baby looks at her making faces, and smiles.

'He smiled at you. That is the first time he smiled at a stranger,' the mother laughs, mutedly. There is great excitement in the household. Mighty shame, thinks Ramani.

The eunuchs pray for the child, and anoint the child's forehead with a special paste of turmeric and saffron. 'The paste will not be washed off, but allowed to disappear gradually,' whispers The Professor.

The head of the household, the fattest man, brings a basket full of good things: sweets, fruit, four bottles of milk, four gold coins and more sweets. Later, at home, they all sit around the table. The supper is good. The sweets are delicious, the milk creamy and the apples crisp. When Ramani drinks the milk, some of the foam stays on her upper lip, which trembles with confusion; confusion between fulfilling her duty ordained at birth and this weird life for which she was destined.

That night, Ramani looks out of her window. It is almost dawn. Ramani must have been standing for at least five full minutes before she sees her: Mother! She sees her mother and sister walking down the road ahead. Ramani charges down the stairs, her heart thumping like a heavy wheelbarrow racing over hard rocks. In the dawn light, she can make out the shadows – she can actually recognize them, after all these years!

'Mother, Mother,' she yells, running after the shadows.

Perhaps that is what the shadows hear; the thumping of a heavy wheelbarrow over hard rocks. The shadows begin to run without stopping. Mother's shadow turns, a precise forty-eight-degree angle.

'Run! Run!' the shadow says, 'there is an ali chasing us!'

Ramani is now out of breath. The Evil One has caught up with her. 'Come home now!' The Evil One commands, brusquely.

Dawn is coming quickly now. And from Ramani's eyes, tears begin to fall. She does not know how many tears her eyes can actually hold. Her tears fall all day. Through her tears, Ramani sees an image that haunts her; a single image, seared in her memory from a melancholic pantomime. When her mother's shadow had turned a precise forty-eight degrees, Ramani had seen the eyes. In those eyes, there had flickered a barely visible flame of recognition. There would be no going home.

The Professor sits at her clinic. She has become a godsend for anyone who is infertile, or has polio. Queues of people wait outside her clinic, patiently. This eunuch represents hope. Time and time again, her prayers have taken their illnesses by surprise; reversed people's failures to procreate. A little girl is brought forward by her parents. She has lost use of her left leg. She has polio. The government vaccinators had come to her village, but her parents were too busy working in the fields to take her to the vaccination centre. Now she walks with a limp; her left leg is almost just skin and bone. The Professor looks at the little girl. This girl has eyes black as charcoal, and curly eyelashes. The Professor lays her hand on the girl's back. She squirts turmeric water on her back and rubs a special paste of crushed leaves on it. The girl squeals as the cold water trickles down her back, to her legs. 'Go home,' The Professor says. 'Your leg will regain its strength in a few weeks.'

One by one, people come forward.

A couple steps up, expectantly. The disease is hidden somewhere between them. They are childless. They have been to several infertility clinics and have had numerous scans. The Professor listens to their story. She closes her eyes and looks up. She sees two storks join together and fly high. They fly high above Madras, circling. The eunuch prays. Her voice sounds bird-like, like a stork's.

'What is it going to be?' they ask. 'Please don't tell us the gods will curse us with a girl.'

The eunuch speaks, still in a bird-like voice. 'It will be the last night of the Tamil year; the night when Tamils throw out the old year and welcome the new one. The night will be dark and quiet. You will hear the voices of storks. And the baby will arrive. Yes, it will be a boy,' she says. The couple prostrate themselves before the eunuch, touching her feet in supplication.

Ramani is not sure what powers The Professor has. But the people keep coming; their feet pound a dusty path to the door of the clinic. The Professor knows what they want, and waits. She goes about her business of healing and curing. Life radically changes for the people she comes across. How can she explain her powers? Or her unsalaried, yet remunerated, presence at the clinic? Of course, she cannot explain her powers. How could she, when the medical doctors and clever scientists cannot explain her powers? She looks at the deity of Lord Ganesha in the corner of the clinic. A single naked light bulb dangles in front of his trunk. She folds her hands and bows down in front of the deity. She thanks him again and again. It is here that, every day, he lends her his powers for a few minutes. Lord Ganesha looks down, expressionless, at the folded hands of the eunuch. His stone eyes look at the tips of her fingers. Surprisingly dainty fingers, for a eunuch, he thinks.

The eunuch stuffs several rupee notes into her small silk purse. She thanks the Lord once more for his daily gratuity. It is the end of the day. She heads home.

The Evil One has brought some music videos home. Ramani likes Michael Jackson. A few years ago he had released his defining album, *Thriller*.

Michael Jackson is difficult to describe. He sings like a castrato and wears make-up like a migrato, she thinks. Over the years, his skin has become lighter. It is like he wants to be a universal being – neither white nor black; neither male nor female; neither boy nor adult. She likes his dancing. She wonders why he calls his characteristic dance the 'moon walk'. His rhythm is silky smooth. Walking on the moon would be difficult with all the bumpy craters. She thinks his dance should have been called the 'glass walk'.

Ramani tries glass walking. She attempts several trial runs before she shows it to the rest. She slides her feet backwards, her heels and forefeet getting a good feel for the floor. After each trial, she stops and measures her glass-walk step by putting her heel to the toe of her other foot.

Slowly, her rhythm improves. The Evil One and The Hooker clap as she completes her routine. 'You'll be dancing at weddings, soon. Except, unlike the usual wedding scenario, they won't ask us to leave. They'll be paying us to stay,' says The Evil One proudly.

Ramani likes glass walking. She finds she is unable to resist her fascination for this dance. The more the others appreciate her skill, the more she feels unparalleled joy, a freedom to appreciate her own ability. She is ashamed that she enjoys the adulation of the other three eunuchs.

The Evil One keeps an eye on the nearby *kalyana mandapam*: the wedding hall. Any new wedding will be gate-crashed, and blessings offered to the couple. The watchman of the *kalyana mandapam* usually gives them notice of advance bookings; for a bribe, of course.

The Professor sees Ramani standing at the window, 'Tonight's the *panda kaal muhurtham,*' The Professor tells her.

'What's that?'

'That happens one day before the wedding. Can you see the bamboo pole there? That is a symbolic representation of a deity. Both families are praying for good fortune, to the bamboo pole. Tomorrow is the wedding. That means we go there tomorrow.'

The sound of a wedding band drifts in through the window. It is still dark outside. Ramani hears the music through the dream clouds and rainbows of her sleep. She opens her eyes, sleepily. What time is it? It must be before six! The auspicious hour, calculated by the astrologer, must have been early that day. Then Ramani hears loud voices, and some dancing. The nadaswaram players are playing loudly, their cheeks puffed in effort. The wedding procession is passing right outside her window. Ramani can hear excerpts of conversation as she lies in bed.

The procession follows the narrow street towards the *kalyana mandapam.* The streets are narrow. The drums carried by the drummers occasionally scrape against the houses in the street. Children, awoken by the din, lean out of their windows, and receive sweets and rice cakes from the crowd. Finally, the procession enters the wedding hall.

Ramani rushes down to The Professor. 'The procession has reached the *mandapam*,' she says. 'The wedding must be today!'

'No, the wedding festivities last for three days. Today is the receiving of the groom. Come with me onto the terrace. We will have a good view from there.'

Ramani sees the groom and his family arrive at the wedding hall. The groom's family is welcomed with a tray containing a lot of flowers. She sees a silver tray holding flowers, pan supari, and fruits. She sees a lady, beautifully decked out in a gold-threaded green sari, sprinkle rose water on the groom. Another lady, probably the bride's mother, garlands the groom and applies vibhuti to his forehead. Some of the sacred ash falls off his forehead onto his cheeks. She offers the groom some sweets.

'They usually give him *paal khoa*, made from condensed milk.'

The priest performs a pooja, the ritual prayer and breaks a coconut, to ward off the evil spirits. It is said that the cracking of the coconut makes the evil spirits lose themselves in a mist.

'What happens next?'

The Professor smiles at Ramani's curiosity. 'The *pallikai thellichal*.'

'What are the people doing?'

'Can you see the clay pots there?'

'There are lots of them.'

'Usually nine; each pot is filled with a different variety of grain. Can you see the women sprinkling water into the pots? The women are from both families, and have to be married. Unmarried women cannot be part of this ritual.'

Ramani watches intently as the sound of lilting veena music reaches her ears. She opens the window to let more music in. The music seems to travel down the narrow street, along the walls of the houses, and climb in through the terrace. Ramani leans out and looks at the houses, the peeling plaster giving them a mottled appearance.

'What is the pond in the *kalyana mandapam* for?'

'By tomorrow, the day of the wedding, these grains will sprout. These nine pots will be immersed in the pond, so the fish there can feed on the grains and bless the newly-weds.'

Ramani is not sure if this explanation is real or not. She hates to admit that she likes The Professor's stories. She sits at the table, having breakfast and thinking about the fish in the pond blessing the wedding couple. She thinks about the fish in the Kaveri River. She used to know almost each and every one of them. Perhaps not every one of them, but she could have almost called them by number. The little ones used to feel bony and hard, but the big ones were fleshy and tender. Kadallaikaran used to wade into the water and catch them in a pan. Thinking about the village makes her remember her sadness. The Professor can see how far away her thoughts are. She does not interrupt Ramani's thoughts. Ramani is quiet all day.

It is the day of the wedding.

Then it is time for them to go to the wedding hall. The Evil One leads this procession of four. They pass the outer wall and enter the compound. Ramani can hear music and the drone of the priest reciting the mantras. The bamboo is still standing in the courtyard from the previous day. Ramani sees it is a female bamboo. The female bamboo still has the roots attached. Female bamboos are more delicate; leaving the roots makes them stay fresh longer. Ramani's eyes fall on the large group of bedecked people. They are family members, facing the couple and participating in the wedding ritual. The priest recites mantras in hard-to-understand Sanskrit. The couple follows him in unison, and at times, in a solo voice. The eyes of the crowd fall on the eunuchs. One of the men comes rushing towards The Evil One.

'Please be leaving. We don't want you to be

making any trouble.'

'We are here to bless the couple. That is our job.'

'Why do you have to come here! Why?' A feeling of anger and frustration shows in his voice. 'How much?'

'Three hundred rupees.'

The man's thick eyebrows and small mouth twitch. His fingers tremble slightly as he unties a bundle of rupee notes. He hands over a small pile without counting it. 'Please go. Leave right now!'

The Evil One takes the money. 'This is a beautiful wedding,' she says. 'May the Lord Ganesha bless this couple abundantly.'

They slowly leave the *kalyana mandapam*. Outside, a few kids are playing. One of them is showing off his dance moves. 'Look, I'm dancing like Michael Jackson!'

Ramani cannot resist. 'That's not how MJ dances.'

The boy looks up, his dance aborted. He goes red and begins to sulk. 'As if a eunuch would know,' he retorts.

Ramani walks up. She raises her hand in an imploring gesture, as if to say, 'Let me dance.' Only a white glove is missing.

Glass walking like Michael Jackson liberates Ramani's soul – not with the all-conquering dream and the all-consuming passion she feels when she flies kites, but with a sense of colourful enjoyment nevertheless.

'She's bloody good,' the boy says admiringly. A small crowd gathers to watch Ramani. They begin clapping. In the stillness of the heat, Ramani's heels swish against the stone floor. She glides and twirls. The crowd keeps asking for more.

'Later,' says Ramani. 'I still have improvements to make.'

She walks with a triumphant air, the crowd still clapping.

The man with the bushy eyebrows is now among the crowd, having come out to see what the commotion was about. He looks at The Evil One, 'Maybe she can dance at our reception?' he gesticulates towards Ramani.

The Evil One smiles. 'Sure. But Ramani is already an established star. Her fee will be a thousand rupees.' With her inexhaustible cunning optimism, she does not fail to take a material interest in the situation. Ramani heads home. She feels good. She likes the interest her dance moves are getting.

Ramani really needs to pee. She sits on the toilet. Strange, she thinks, even when she was a boy she used to sit and pee. For some reason, the foreskin used to spray the pee all over the toilet floor otherwise. Maybe it was because the foreskin was long. Kumar used to tease Raman about it. It had reached a stage where peeing always had to be behind a closed door. That was in her previous life. She longs for her old friends.

Muslim boys are lucky. They have no foreskin. And they have a brick at home. They had a Muslim boy in class, Nazir. One day Ramani had seen a brick in the toilet in Nazir's house. Nazir explained that it was for the 'golden drop'. With no foreskin, he used to say, you can't shake urine fully off your sunni. There is always a drop that lingers on the underside – the golden drop. Menfolk in the house touch their sunnis on the brick after peeing. The brick absorbs the drop, he said.

Ramani wonders why she had never learnt to pee standing up. Perhaps that was a sign of things to come. Perhaps that was her karma, her fate.

She sees a boy flying a kite in the distance. She misses flying kites. They are her first passion. Kites are easy to make. They don't move unless you move. But give them some air and they take on a mind of their own, a defiant spirit. Kites are like windows to her soul, she thinks; like multicoloured glass windows. There is a church close by. It has multicoloured stained-glass windows. Every Sunday she looks through the window; the people in the church look different in different colours. Through the red glass, the church looks like a furnace, breathing fiery sermons. Through the green glass, the church looks like a forest, each person a tree in the forest of faith. Through the yellow glass, the church looks bathed in gold, filled with the congregation's riches. Ramani is amazed at how many different moods a multicoloured glass window has; like a kite.

She finds a newspaper. She begins to cut out the shape of a kite. Then she stops. She knows it is a mistake. Kites need freedom. She will never fly a kite until she is truly free.

Kites are unique. Virtually any toy or ball can be thrown up into the sky. They all fall down again, almost immediately; except for kites. Kites want to listen to the wind tell stories. Sometimes the wind makes up different voices. 'Just finish the story,' the kites seem to say. Kites don't mind different voices. Love has many different voices.

The next morning, Ramani wakes early. She looks out the window, to see if any kites are flying. Even in her sleep, she hears whispers – the wind telling stories to kites. She hears many soft inaudible whispers. Today we go to the *kalyana mandapam* again, she thinks.

Back at the *mandapam*, Ramani has a surprise. Just as she enters the outer wall, she sees herself confronting a large swing, a structure erected specifically for the purpose of the wedding. Lining the frame of the swing are numerous light bulbs, like raindrops in the night sky. 'What's the swing for?' she asks.

'You'll see, soon,' The Professor tells her.

The couple are garlanding themselves thrice, completing their marriage. They move towards where Ramani is standing and sit on the swing. All unmarried women are asked to move aside; the eunuchs also step aside. Married women from the invited families feed the couple spoonfuls of milk and banana pieces. They pick up clumps of rice grains and fling them high up in circular motion. The rice grains fly high, some getting lodged in the crevices of the ceiling. The rice droppings, as they fall, cast an almost phosphorescent white on the stone floor. Then the *oonjal pattu*, the 'song of the swing', begins. The song is clear. It is loud, but no one covers their ears. People listen, captivated by the chorus. No one sees the bride stand up suddenly. The swing shudders slightly as she stands.

The bride disappears. When she re-enters the scene, she is wearing a nine-yard sari. The number 9 signifies the union of the male and the female; one and cipher; Shiva and Shakti.

The bride's father sits in the centre of the room, his face sombre. His daughter now sits on his lap, as he sits on a sack of paddy. Paddy symbolizes good fortune and wealth. For many years he has imagined this moment. Just as he had worked his paddy fields, his daughter had worked for him, reigning over his one hundred acres. There is nothing on his farm, not even the goats, that she has not presided over. Now she is leaving, for a new home. He sighs. That is life, he thinks; filled with bittersweet impermanence. He looks down at the crisp folds of his daughter's long sari. He picks up the yoke from his plough, and hands it over to the priest. He can see some soil from his farm still on the yoke. The yoke is touched to his daughter's forehead. He hopes that the couple will always walk together, pulling the plough of life.

The priest blesses the mangalasutra, the sacred thread, and gives it to the groom. The groom picks up the sacred thread and places it on his bride's neck, tying two knots. He stops short of tying the third and final knot. He must never tie the third knot, or risk bad fortune. The drums begin to roll. The sound of drums echoes across the room. The groom stands

89

there, frozen in an unspoken rule of ceremony. His sister steps forward. She ties the third knot on the sacred thread. One, two, and three: season after season, each knot represents a specific union – the union of the threesome: mind, body and spirit.

This is not a basic act of betrothal. Knot after knot has to be tied properly, an uninterrupted act of marital union. Nothing can disturb or interfere with the specific order of a Tamil wedding.

Then it is time for Ramani to dance at the reception. Gradually she feels her energy shifting into the rhythm of her dance. The guests clap as she glass walks, egging her on. She needs no egging on. She whirls around, in a mad spin – one dance move replacing another in a perfect carousel. The crowd stands stupefied by the inexhaustibility of her fierce energy.

6

OVER A DECADE has simply disappeared, she thinks. The desire to escape has never left Ramani; from a desire it has developed into an obsession. Seasons have passed and new moons have risen. Tides have changed. Although she gets on with the business of living, a loneliness and despair always lingers.

She reminds herself to be civil, to familiarize herself with this world of eunuchs – after all, this might help with what she calls 'the education of escape'. She watches from the roof terrace as a policeman enters the video store at the front of the harem.

The Evil One smiles, showing a row of misshapen stained teeth.

'How many customers do you have?' the policeman asks.

'A hundred and twelve each week, and two are women,' she replies.

The policeman looks at the eunuch. His eyes briefly study the sturdy legs, uncrossed. He counts the membership cards.

'Look. I am just doing my duty,' he says. 'Do you have any porn videos in your store?'

The Evil One smiles again. 'Of course not.' She slips the policeman a hundred-rupee bill. The policeman salutes her and disappears. She glances at the back of the disappearing policeman and clicks her fingers. From the back of the shop, customers come out of hiding. They push open a hidden ramshackle door and enter the main room, stacked with shelves. Each shelf stores dozens of porn videos. Four young men eagerly look through the videos.

'What do you recommend?' they ask the eunuch.

'Depends what you want. If you want rape, I've got a real good one. It's called *I Spit on Your Grave*. It has great rape scenes of this girl and then she takes revenge and kills each one of the rapists. It's bloody great! I've got some local porn too – some secret videos of our local Tamil actresses, shot in beach resorts at Mahabalipuram.'

The young men listen to The Evil One in absorbed silence, taking in the information. They are young fellows, of between twenty and twenty-five. Most of them are smoking and two of them keep spitting on the floor. Each one of the boys picks a video. The last one of the men, the oldest fellow, picks *I Spit on Your Grave*.

'Can I watch it here?' he asks.

'That will be extra – twenty rupees for the booth.'

The Evil One sits calmly, smoking and waiting for the video to be over. The other young men have left. She hears the background music of the porn video – grunts and screams, an occasional expectoration, hollow coughing and heavy breathing. Then the young man emerges, sweating. 'That was fucking great!' he says.

The eunuch barely acknowledges him. She is busy arranging the desk, gathering the video library cards and counting the earnings. She is satisfied. It is the end of the day.

What else is she to do? At least she has a business. Her girls are all doing well. Kamalam makes good money treating infertile couples and Mira turns good tricks. She needs to find some work for the new girl, Ramani. The welfare of her girls comes first. After her time, they need to be able to look after themselves. The new girl still does not understand why she is amongst us, she thinks. After all, what was done was out of necessity, sanctified by ancient Indian tradition. Everyone knows eunuchs are necessary, and have magic powers. All birth is traumatic. A child is born with blood and tears. Eunuchs are born with blood and tears, too. If she had not adopted Ramani, their household would have been incomplete.

She leaves the store and walks towards Marina Beach. She stands and admires the seagulls. A few young boys follow her, calling her names. She turns and lifts her skirt, threatening to expose her genitals. The boys flee, terrified.

'Shit! Run! Run! *Ayyo! Ayyo!* She is a eunuch! She is going to curse us and make us impotent.'

The Evil One sits calmly on the sand, admiring the magnificent majesty of the sea. The salty sea air seems strangely sardonic. She smiles at the receding shadows of the fleeing boys.

Kiran Chand spots Rajinder sitting on the sand. He is from North India and has lived in Madras for years. He is a developer of apartment blocks.

'How's it going?' he greets her.

'Good. What about you?

'I've almost completed my new project "Marina Gardens" – four towers and 400 flats,' he gesticulates towards the grandiose building nearby.

Rajinder looks at the towers. 'How much?'

'Same deal. You dance and bless each room to take away the *drishti*, the bad luck. Every other time I have been lucky, with your help – no problems with leaky buildings or tenants. This time I have increased your payment to a thousand rupees a tower.'

'Fuck off,' she says. 'Seeing that you are my first apartment for this month, *bohni* money will be an extra two thousand per apartment tower, or no deal.'

Kiran Chand agrees. It might be a twisted inducement, but he cannot afford bad luck on his buildings. This eunuch has brought him much luck – and much money. He would be foolish to refuse the extra money for the first job of the month.

Rajinder wanders to the southern corner of the beach. There are a few dunes here. This will be her watch. She will have to watch Mira, until the end of the night.

The Hooker walks down the main strip of the beach. She wears a bright red sari tucked up at the waist. She is fair-skinned and slender and cuts quite a figure on the beach. It is late. The beach is littered with couples seeking privacy, and other hookers.

Mira is tall and has long black hair. When she smiles, she is dangerously irresistible. She feels she has the fortune of good looks that the other hookers on the beach cannot match. After all, in the scheme of things, eunuchs are usually cheaper than 'straight' hookers; not Mira, though. When clients ask for a hooker at the Star Hotel nearby, the manager always offers them the option of a eunuch at half price. That makes her so mad, she wants to cry. She is different. She asks twice the rate of a normal hooker. Unlike the other hookers, she walks behind the sailing club, where the gentlemen with the money go. Only classy hookers go there.

Mira walks along the beach behind the sailing club. She sees some fishermen hauling in a big fishing net. There are nine men, all tugging and heaving together. They are good-looking men, with neatly trimmed beards. They look like they are from Kerala, or perhaps further up the Malabar Coast. Local fishermen here have unkempt beards.

'Ale ale ey il asah,' they keep chanting in unison as they haul the fishing nets. The biggest one, at the front, leads the chorus. The fishing net is like a cape on his shoulders. Like a caped crusader, he seems to be hauling the sea into the sand. With each heave the chorus goes up: *Ale ale ey il asah.* Their voices have a deep baritone, and their chant epitomizes teamwork, loyalty and strength.

The fish skins glisten in the moonlight, the tails flap and leap into the air. There is no escape for a fish, in this life. The rules of human life are the same. Eunuchs, once taken from their families, have no escape from fate; at least not in this lifetime. Rajinder told her that she was chosen by the gods to be a eunuch. There are a million eunuchs in India 'chosen' from their families, never to return to family life; like the fish in the net, Mira thinks.

The smell of the sea and the fish has risen all the way to the moon, and Mira forgets her sadness. She sees a gentleman drinking some broth. Actually, he has had too much broth and his head is not straight. He is like an octopus on the bottom of the ocean; his movements random and uncoordinated. He will be easy, she thinks. He won't last long.

'*Kaia vaia, pathu ruba*' ('Hand or mouth, ten rupees'), she says.

'Mouth,' he mumbles, trying to unbutton his fly.

'Here, let me help you,' she offers.

He sees her kneel down and her hair cascades over her back like a big black wave. Her gentle fair skin stands out against the darkness of her hair. She senses that he wants her mouth. *All* married men want mouth. She slides her hand between his thighs, gently squeezes him. He feels a strange sensation of weakness, an uncontrollable immobility and he spurts several times. She turns her face aside as his ejaculate lands on the sand and she can feel shudders passing through his thighs.

'I'm sorry,' he apologizes. 'I came too soon. You won't tell anyone?'

'That'll cost you twenty extra,' she says in a matter-of-fact kind of way. He pulls out his wallet and completes the transaction. Men are easy. She spies a young man. Well dressed. She has seen him here before, driving a pleasure and parking it way down the road so no one will know him. He looks at her nervously.

'Hi, there,' she says.

'Are you available?'

'You look nice and clean. Special discount for you, fifty rupees,' she says.

He thinks of haggling, but the beautiful force of her body unleashes itself on him. The softness of her hands and the suppleness of her flesh clear his indecision. He feels his muscle harden as he responds to her.

'You're so strong,' she says. Men like hearing that. He tries to embrace her. He tries to hold her face and kiss her. She turns her mouth away slightly and lets him kiss her cheeks. He gets warm and she takes off his trousers and lays them down on the sand. He is naked on the sand, and she positions their bodies far enough to avoid the caress of the sea. She holds his kipper and rubs it between her legs. He lets her guide him. With magical sleight of hand, she greases him and guides him between her legs. This young man does not know where his sunni is, but does not care as long as he gets off his *thongattans*, she thinks. The sensation is delicious. His sunni may as well be in the sand. He opens his eyes wide and sees her below him, her dark hair scattered among the sand crests. He tries to stay balanced, but her beauty overpowers him. A grunt of amazement rushes out of him, as she grabs him harder and gives him the ride of his life. Then Mira sees a man walking around. He is wearing some uniform, some kind of chauffeur uniform. 'My boss wants you,' he says. 'You will have to come with me to his house, though.'

Mira remembers what Rajinder says about leaving the beach. Never leave the beach! she has been told. The seaside is a haven for eunuchs. Tonight Mira feels confident. After all, she is elegant and pretty, not like the shabby hookers. This man must be a politician or a film star to have a uniformed chauffeur. She has always longed to be chauffeured in a pleasure.

She leans back on the seat and trusts the impetuously speeding vehicle.

Rajinder is busy dancing and blessing the apartments at 'Marina Gardens'. She does not see Mira leave the beach.

Back at the house, Ramani and The Professor stand

on the terrace. The terrace is bathed in moonlight. Standing there, looking at the moon, Ramani remembers the night-time kite flying in the village. The silver moon hangs like an oval kite on the night sky. Huddled next to the moon, and shimmering against the night sky, are the stars.

The Professor looks up at the moon. 'The pale moonlight is an artist, an illusionist,' she says. 'It chips away at the outer skin of people's faces, and like a razor pares away at the rough spots.'

They look up at the moon. Everyone knows the moon has many craters, but they can see none. Ramani looks at The Professor. Her face is bathed in a glow, and her pores and acne scars no longer visible. The moonlight has brightened her face down to a smoothness.

Ramani thinks of the village moon, on the banks of the Kaveri River.

The moon beautifies faces, Kadallaikaran used to say. 'That is why in English films, every fellow falls in love in the moonlight. Here in the village, girls are not seen out at night. That is why men get dowry when they marry.'

It is the first time for Mira in the back of a car all by herself. She longs to ask the chauffeur to take the long route but she does not want to cut into her profits. It seems about half an hour and the pleasure stops in front of a lamp post. The driver asks her to get out. He accompanies her to a big house. The politician looks at her. 'I am glad you are here,' he says. 'I pay good money and give things to eat and drink. I've foreigners here with me. They tell me they like high-toned people and people who dress like dancers. You are going to make us all very happy,' he laughs.

He smells of onions and his gut is repulsive. Sometimes clients are not very clean and she has to service them, but she never does more than one at a time. She wants to say, 'OK, I had a ride in your pleasure car but please let me go.' And then she sees that she is going to be in the company of five men, and everything has been prepared for her to be alone with them for the whole night. The men tug at her clothes. 'Let me go, you beasts, or I will curse you!' she yells. She can see four of the men are foreign, and not well versed with Indian tradition. They do not fear a eunuch. Her fear seems to excite them further. She struggles to get free. 'I like prostitutes with some fighting spirit,' one of them smirks. They grab her and carry her upstairs. Two of them hold her down on the floor, while they penetrate her every orifice. Every time she resists, she is slapped and raped again. They call her a eunuch slut. They end up in a circle around her spitting and kicking her, until she is curled up in pain and covered with bruises. One of them tries to shove a bottle up her anus. Mira's screams echo into the night. At the beach, with the intuition of a mother, Rajinder feels every scream like a dagger in her heart.

Mira is awake. She is home. She has been carried home by Rajinder, who found her lying unconscious on the beach. There are muffled sounds around her. Ramani and Kamalam are taking turns at mopping her brow. She tries to call out to them, but no sound escapes her lips.

'Shh, sweetheart,' Kamalam says. 'Everything will be all right. You are home now.'

Mira remembers nothing, for a long time. Then she remembers riding in the pleasure car, the big house and the men. She shudders and remembers the pain and the humiliation. She lies in the dim light, listening. Her back and thighs hurt. She feels a searing pain in her bottom. Ramani catches her pained expression and holds her close. She stirs to allow Ramani more room in the bed. This is the first time Ramani has given her a hug, she thinks.

Rajinder has disappeared. They both wonder where Rajinder is.

Rajinder is walking the streets. It is almost dawn and the moon has gone to sleep. The street lamps still glow orange against the dawn air. Rajinder walks briskly, like a crab on the sand, her feet barely touching the ground. She feels anger. She checks her bag to make sure she has a handkerchief; and her knife. She scours driveway after driveway until she spots the politician's car. She follows the driver as he walks towards the politician's house, after locking the car. The driver sees nothing; except signs. The signs say: 'Expired', 'Deceased', 'Passed away'.

The driver does not see the shadow amongst the bushes. Rajinder adjusts her handkerchief on her nose, forming a mask. The driver feels a short sharp pain between his shoulder blades. He sees a face covered by a handkerchief covering his mouth. Then the signs disappear, and he feels nothing.

Rajinder enters the room. The room is like a room in a movie show, with velvet chairs and walls dark as the souls inhabiting the house. She feels her temples throb, her skin pulses as she moves towards the stairs, stealthily. There is a lamp burning at the top of the stairs. The stairs have a coir carpet. She feels nausea and an anger rise as she ascends the stairs.

She sees four men sleeping, drunk. She moves without noise. Then fury overcomes her. Her hands and arms seem to separate from her as they take the knife out of her bag. She watches her hands as if they are possessed. Her hands now have a mind of their own – they smash the men's cheekbones, and slash their throats. Bones crunch and their bedclothes saturate with blood. The men lie without moving, like broken dolls, a deathly gurgle in their throats. She counts the bodies: four. Foreigners; the politician is not here, she thinks.

Just then, someone grabs her from behind. 'What do you think you are doing in my house?'

Surprising him with her speed, she kicks him in the groin, doubling him over. Once again her hands take over her mind, as fear takes over his. Clothes tear as she rips his *veshti* with her knife, exposing his thighs.

'Bitch! You kill me and it will be all over the papers. They will arrest you before you can say eunuch shit!'

'Killing is too good for you,' she says. 'You need to suffer for what you have done.'

He tries to rise up. He is powerless against this crazed eunuch. She pushes him against the wall. Shit! She's strong.

How much pain must he be made to feel to avenge Mira's pain? Rajinder wonders. Is it better to just kill him? She must make sure that he can never hurt another as he has hurt Mira. There must be a better way. She grabs the knife and stabs him in the stomach. She sees blood spurt from the wound as he roars in pain. She jerks the knife downwards, slicing his underpants. Then she makes an incision, the practised incision of the eunuch. She looks at his cowering self with pity. 'You will never be able to make love to your wife and she will scorn you. You will never be able to tell anyone the truth or your political career is over. And if you complain to the police that you were castrated by a eunuch, they'll say they have seen this happen before a thousand times, but they will not arrest a eunuch lest bad luck befalls their families. So, Mr. Politician, I don't give a shit. I have not murdered you and you are a castrato, but no court in the land will touch me. As for your friends, you'd better clean up the mess or you will have some explaining to do.'

She reaches into her bag and takes out a bottle. She opens the lid. The politician smells a strong-smelling liquid. He sees the eunuch wander among the carcasses of the four foreigners. He is powerless to do anything. Barely conscious, he does not know what she is doing.

As Rajinder walks out of the politician's house, she prays to Lord Ganesha. 'May you soften my heart and dry my bloodthirsty eyes so that I will no longer thirst for revenge,' she says.

She hears a clap of thunder. 'Thank you, Lord Ganesha,' she says.

Back at the house, Mira lies in bed, thinking herself awake. She remembers the face of the politician and the foreigners. Did they savage her because they knew she was weak and powerless? Or because they wanted to share their ugliness with her? Ramani sits by her side constantly. At times she goes away to bring her water, and idlis and chutney wrapped in newspapers. Mira nibbles at one of the rice cakes. Mira catches Ramani looking at her. The look is loving, appraising and nurturing. 'Sleep, my sister, sleep,' Ramani sings, as she threads her fingers through Mira's thick black hair.

It is almost morning. Ramani fights sleep. She wonders where The Evil One is. This is the first time The Evil One has not been home at night. She considers escaping. This is a perfect opportunity. She looks at Mira lying bruised and battered next to her. She looks at her face, now turning purple with bruising. For a moment, she is charged with a difficult task: to suppress her impulse to escape and be there for her sister. She looks with love at Mira. In the eyes of the world they are eunuchs, but she knows their love has the dignity of sisterhood. Ramani hears the door bang and stiffens. The Evil One must be back. A brief notion of fear comes upon her. I should have run away when I had the chance, she thinks. Then for some time she hears nothing. Then she hears footfalls.

She remembers The Evil One whispering, 'Is she all right?'

Ramani nods. 'Still in a lot of pain and has a lot of bruises.'

Mira stirs. Ramani sees The Evil One look at her. The Evil One has a pained expression. 'I am sorry, Mira. I am sorry I could not protect you. I failed you.'

'It's not your fault. If I had listened to you and not left the beach . . .'

'Shush, my daughter. You will never go to the beach at night. In the daytime you can go, as you love the sea. You can listen to the sea speak, and watch the crabs dance. But I will never let anyone touch you again.'

The Evil One puts her hand into the bag. She feels loathing and disgust. It is almost too much; the jar in her bag makes her feel nauseous. She feels anger that she has let Mira down. Her heart beats – a hammering knot of muscle.

'I have something to show you.'

Mira sits up. Ramani props a pillow under her.

'How many men did you say there were?'

The memory seems too painful. 'Five,' she croaks.

The Evil One lifts up the large bottle to the light. The light falls on the formalin in the jar. In it float five penises and five pairs of testicles.

'Mira, my daughter. I promise you that no one will even come near you again.' Mira takes the jar. She puts the jar on the bedside table. 'Thank you,' she says, kissing Rajinder's hand.

Ramani asks, 'Will they come to live with us now?'

Rajinder looks at Ramani, stunned by the innocence of the question. 'No sweet one,' she says. 'Criminals will never belong in the world of eunuchs. That is not acceptable to us. And Lord Ganesha would never allow that. My duty is to look after my girls.'

Ramani never thinks of her as The Evil One again.

7

HANDS, KUMAR THINKS. Every moment that has defined him has to do with his hands. When he flies his kites, or prepares the manja, it is all done with his hands. Now here he is; the proud owner of Cool Cut, his very own barber salon. Now his hands hold the scissors which delicately work through hair, like a plough through a field. Right now, his hands trace the curve of a particular chin with shaving foam.

His clients are lucky. For ten rupees they can be shorn of hair. They can listen to the radio and escape from the Madras heat in the air-conditioned comfort. They can discuss politics and understand the vision of the ADMK party. One of the clients asks him if the kite on the wall is his. That is the kite he had made twelve years ago in the village of KKP. He had cut up several newspapers and had made a diamond-shaped collage. He tells the client that the kite is his. He does not tell the client that he has not flown a kite for twelve years; that he does not want to fly this kite ever again; that he has never been back to his village.

He looks at the kite on the wall.

Has it really been twelve years since he flew that kite with Lakshmi, the night before she killed herself? He had held her in his arms and she had flown his kite. That was the happiest moment of his life, which had become shortlived.

He looks at the kite again, emblazoned with the words 'I LOVE YOU' in red ink.

He had found the kite caught among the trees and dripping wet. The ink had smudged slightly. He had looked for Lakshmi in vain, together with all the people in the village. She was gone.

He now lives in Madras. He opened Cool Cut eight years ago. He looks at the framed kite on the wall. He looks at the various newspaper clippings which had made up the collage. There are clippings from hundreds of different newspapers stuck on the piece of paper at random, which was how he had made the kite. Kadallaikaran used to say that yesterday's newspaper stories have to move forward even if they have no destination. Their letters dance and change the meaning of words; dreams become nightmares and nightmares become dreams. Kumar keeps looking at the newspaper. He looks at the different newspaper clippings pasted side by side, overlapping at the edges in different patterns. Words added to words have no more meaning than stitches on a patchwork quilt. Then suddenly a sentence stands out. Sure, it is a sentence where words from different newspaper clippings have formed a line. It reads: GIRL. FOUND. IN. KAVERI RIVER. LIVES. ADOPTED BY NUNS. AT. LADIES SEAT. WHEELCHAIR.

Surely the words have rearranged themselves. How could he not have read this line while making the kite? It would have made no sense then, he thinks.

This little sense of clarity brings with it nausea and fear, and he is seized by a cold sweat. Here hangs a kite which was made twelve years ago, out of a random pile of newspapers.

Kadallaikaran was right. Yesterday's stories did dance and change their words. If he is right, could a nightmare become a dream?

He is disturbed by this thought. Looking at it logically, it makes no sense to think this way. He is probably stupid for taking this seriously. Nevertheless, he goes to the local post office, and a postal clerk tells him that Ladies Seat does indeed exist; and that it is in Yercaud, high up in the Shevaroy Hills. The Shevaroy Hills rise magnificently outside Salem; that would make Ladies Seat a three-hour bus trip from his old village.

Thoughts of Lakshmi come back. They seem perfectly natural, even though he has not allowed himself to think about her for twelve years.

In his mind he can see a girl with a rather handsome face and wide brown eyes. In her beautiful smile he sees a trace of constraint and sadness. She is slightly built and almost as tall as him. Her lips are full. Her hair is long, almost to her butt.

He imagines walking with her by the Kaveri River, after flying kites. Conversation is spasmodic and difficult. As the river breeze gets colder at night, it loosens their tongues and they speak more. He remembers saying something that makes her laugh; and that he is charmed by the sweetness of her laughter.

Then she sits down beside him. His memory is a bit sketchy on the details now, but he remembers her soft hand on his. He remembers her kissing his cheek in the all-embracing darkness, which wipes away her shyness and constraint.

The next day, she is gone. He remembers looking for her. His eyes search the four corners of the village and the river bank. Then, he spots the kite; *his* kite. He sees her writing on it. He holds the kite close. He tries to take with him the warmth of her voice and her perfume, which is like a kurinji flower. He remembers trying to hold on to the smell in his nose, but eventually it withers away, like a kurinji flower eventually does.

He never flies that kite again. That is the kite on the wall of his salon.

He realizes how frighteningly close to the surface her memory is, in spite of everything that has happened. Could she be alive?

Kumar returns to KKP after an absence of twelve years. His mission is to get to the Shevaroy Hills and to Ladies Seat, which is the highest point on the mountain.

He waits at the KKP bus station. A few new bus berths, but strangely nothing much has changed in two decades. Everyone local knows that to get a seat on the mountain bus one must bribe Govinda. The bus usually arrives at the bus station fully laden, all the forty seats taken. From behind a tree, a man approaches Kumar. His clothes are the colour of the earth here – a reddish brown.

'*Saar*, you want seat reserved on mountain bus?'

'Govinda? . . . Hell, you look *younger*.'

'You must have known my Dad.'

It makes sense to Kumar – why would Govinda's son not follow in his father's footsteps?

'How much?'

'*Saar*, you are my first customer. I must add *bohni* money – for good luck, *saar*.'

'Twenty rupees.'

'*Saar*, you obviously have not been in the village for a long time. You have become a city man. Now the going rate is a hundred rupees.'

'Twenty-five, then.'

'You drive a hard bargain, s*aar*. But as you are my first customer, and knew my Dad, I'll give you a discount – thirty for you.'

Thirty rupees it is!

Govinda spies a couple of American gentlemen standing nearby.

'From America? Waiting for the mountain bus?'

'How did you know we are Americans?'

Americans are easy to spot. They are full of self-importance and complaints. Everything seems too slow, or dirty, or inefficient for them. One wonders why they bother to travel overseas at all. Kumar sees one of the Americans haggle with Govinda and settle for a discounted sum of two hundred rupees! He grabs one of their bags. The older of the gentlemen, the tall skinny one with the glasses, holds on to his bag. Kumar interrupts their tug-of-war. 'It's OK, Govinda is not a thief; he needs your bag to reserve a seat for you before the bus arrives here.'

Govinda disappears with their bags. About ten minutes later, the bus arrives. A throng of humanity rushes to meet the bus before it has a chance to stop.

On both sides of the bus are men climbing in through the windows, briefly using the still-turning wheels for footholds. Kumar sees reflected shadows of the people on the sides of the bus, momentarily disturbed by the diesel fumes belching from the exhaust on its right side. The driver toots a loud horn to scare away a donkey which has wandered into the bus station amid all the confusion. People regard the moving bus with familiar interest, and immediately try to squeeze through the doors without waiting for the people to disembark. The donkey tries to get in too. The man standing behind the donkey feels its wrath on his kneecap. He howls and falls to the ground, clutching at his knee. The milling crowd steps over him as they converge on the doors of the bus. Kumar can see Govinda smiling at him from the rear of the bus. 'Get in! Get in!' he bellows. The bus is finally at a standstill.

The Americans look puzzled. 'Follow me,' Kumar says, as he hoists himself onto a rear tyre and climbs in through the window. The tall skinny one follows him. His long limbs are bent like a grasshopper's as he tries to fit them through the open window; perhaps not exactly like a grasshopper, maybe more like a praying mantis.

His friend follows suit. By now the donkey has lost interest in boarding the bus, his confusion cleared by a baton-wielding policeman. Kumar is on his way to Yercaud; on his way to Ladies Seat!

Twelve years! The trees have turned from white to green to brown in the mountains. The bus ploughs precariously up the winding mountain roads. The Yercaud Lake levels ebb and rise – flowers lean over the banks and jostle to see their reflection in the pale green waters.

The kurinji flower has bloomed, once. Once? Yes, the kurinji flower only blooms every twelve years – and here it is resplendent in the lattice of leaves. The blueness of the flower is breathtaking. It is as if nature has taken twelve years to decide, to contemplate the range of the blue palette, before it has settled on this precise shade of blue. It is said that the local tribal folk aim to conceive during the kurinji blossom, so that the next blossom will signal the blossoming into womanhood of their daughters. Local funeral litanies still beg forgiveness for the sin of plucking a kurinji flower. The musk of the eucalyptus tree nearby caresses his nose. Kumar feels at home. He has spent large portions of the previous decade in the big smoky city.

The bus climbs up the mountain. The hairpin bends seem endless, and the sun mercilessly bright. The driver does not talk. He is an extension of the beast he is driving, sometimes cursing and swearing, his hands vigorously turning the steering wheel.

Kumar sees the village woman in front of him retch and lean out of the window. 'Drop the shutter of your window!' he screams to the tall American – the one who looks like a praying mantis.

He hesitates. 'Why?'

The woman with motion sickness vomits; her vomit is blown back by the wind through the window onto the American's face. He attempts to clean his glasses with his fingers. Now he knows why! Sometimes local knowledge is all-important. Kumar scrutinizes the American's face. He sits with a bowed head, disgusted.

Finally, the bus arrives in the township atop the hill. Life here is good. People are simple and easy to talk to. They have time for strangers, and their own. Kumar wants to sit by the lake and dream, let his imagination stray to far horizons. But today he must hurry to Ladies Seat.

There is a man, engrossed in cleaning a gate. The gate is made of iron, venerable and rusty.

'Excuse me. Is this the convent at Ladies Seat?'

The man smiles. 'It was the last time I looked.' He adds, 'This convent was founded over a hundred years ago.'

'Wow. This gate dates back one hundred years? It does look a bit crumbly!'

'Crumbly only on the outside – like the nuns here.'

'Are there nuns here?' Kumar asks.

'Of course. In the early 1990s the nuns sold the large abbey building to the girls' school here and some of the land. They kept the cemetery, a few extra acres and moved to a smaller building making it a convent for some enclosed contemplatives.'

'Enclosed contemplatives?'

'Yes, this is the famous Carmelite convent at Ladies Seat. It houses many enclosed contemplatives – nuns that have taken the vow of silence,' the man explained.

Kumar walks towards the stone building.

Kumar sees a nun with an air of superiority. He thinks she might be the mother superior. He rushes up to her.

'Please. Lakshmi . . . the girl who was found in the Kaveri . . . is she here?' he stammers.

The nun is thoughtful. This young man knows Lakshmi's real name. They had never revealed it to anyone. How could he know her name?

'Will she talk to me?' he continues. 'Tell her I am Kumar, an old friend.' Kumar tells the nun his story; his theory.

'And this is because you saw these words on a kite?' she asks, when he has finished.

'Yes.'

Kumar's desperate pleas linger. They caress the air. The nun feels a breeze on her face. This young man has love in his heart, tears in his soul. Perhaps she must ask the young girl. She has always known the girl would never make a nun.

'She has not spoken in years. Wait here,' she directs him.

She disappears. The breeze changes; it is now harsher and more turbulent. Kumar can see the nun walking towards the next building. He struggles to hear above the silence. A burst of impatience threatens to overwhelm him. He resists the urge to run after the nun. His impatience wafts across the sky. A thundercloud disturbs the silence; angrily stamping its hooves on the evening sky. Birds fly from the trees, distressed, looking for refuge. There is an interminable pause – like someone has pressed the pause button on a video recorder, until the picture blurs.

Then, quiet footsteps.

Kumar sees the nun pushing a wheelchair towards him.

Lakshmi?

The girl in the wheelchair looks at him. He is

heading towards her refuge, effacing her walls. None of the abbey's rules now apply.

She looks down at herself. She looks at the wheelchair. She looks up at him through her wide brown eyes. 'Hey, kite flyer,' he says. Just like that.

She smiles. The nun smiles; she has never seen the young girl smile before.

'Why did you come?'

'I had to find you.'

'I am sorry.'

'For what?'

'For not trying to find you. For being a cripple in a wheelchair.'

'It doesn't matter. I'm here.'

'Do you live close by?'

'No, I own my own barber salon in Madras,' Kumar says proudly.

'And Raman?'

'Remember he went to Madras? I tried to find him, but I never heard from him.'

He looks around. The wheelchair is being pushed by the nun. Lakshmi wears a floral blue-and-white salwar kameez. Her long hair is pulled back in a plait. She looks peaceful and the years appear to fall off her. The nun does not steer the wheelchair very well. It bumps into things.

Lakshmi has a radiant smile. Her brown eyes still

have a sparkle, like memories of a wonderful dream. They also hold a sadness, like a haunting past.

His memories go back to a time several years ago. Twelve years ago.

Twelve years with no contact.

He studies her intently. She smiles. Sensing his puzzlement at finding her in a wheelchair, she motions with her hands, asking him to take over the task of pushing the chair. The nun lets him steer. Kumar realizes steering a wheelchair is not that easy. He is not much better than the nun at this task; actually, he is a lot worse.

Night is falling.

'Let's go out and look at the moon,' she says. He pushes the wheelchair out of the room. They go out into the moonlight, the wheelchair wobbling over the cobblestones. It seems to him that the moon has been witness to their greatest joys; and seeing the moon again brings all the warmth right back.

He takes her hands in his. They are cold and thin and he kisses them. She appears moved, still hesitant and unsure. She is silent.

Kumar is also silent, for a moment.

'Lakshmi, what happened to you?'

She sighs. 'When I jumped into the Kaveri River, I broke my spine on a rock.'

Kumar wants to ask why, but he thinks there is

plenty of time for that.

After a brief moment of hesitation she continues. 'Well, the surgeons have told me I will never walk again. Please, Kumar, I think you should go. You will only be disappointed.'

Kumar leads her towards the lake. He is not sure who is doing the leading – they are in unison, their souls entwined. He touches her neck and passes the palm of his hand down the length of her back, to feel her scars. He feels the undulating roughness of the cicatrix. He can feel areas where the scar has stretched leaving small craters. 'Am I hurting you?'

She does not answer. But she does not draw away. With every touch, she seems to relax. Her face glows and her eyes sparkle in the moonlight. She does not speak. He feels her love – *their* love.

'Still flying kites?'

'Last one I flew was with you. I have that kite, though.'

'You found it!' She brightens.

They look up and see fireflies. There are thousands. They remember Gowrie teacher telling them that it is only the male firefly that emits light. Did she say the male firefly dies after copulation? Maybe that was the male mosquito.

He pushes the wheelchair slowly.

Kumar thinks the lake is amazing. Rivers have a

constant flow of life and youthful energy. A sea breathes, and seems knowledgeable and protective. A lake is different. It reflects everything you feel. It is as if it changes its attitude based on yours. It remembers neither bitterness nor insult. The water is stagnant, not mobile; yet its soul is warm and accommodating.

They reach the edge of the lake. They look over the edge and see their reflection in the large wavy mirror. They hold each other close. They are both seized with a feeling that overcomes them, without being prepared for it. The wheelchair now moves in his hands like an obedient mare; he moves it right or left, as he pleases. Now it seems to listen to his command.

He has not felt happiness like this in a long time. They both feel an ecstasy that is greater than their combined love, or happiness.

'Lakshmi, will you marry me?'

'Are you crazy? I'm in a wheelchair. You need your head examined! You don't know lots of things about me.'

'I know enough. I know you fly kites.'

'Badly.'

'Lakshmi, Kadallaikaran used to say that being married was like having a shave – that in the beginning it is nice and smooth, until it reaches the bumpy Adam's apple.'

'So?'

'Maybe we started with the bumpy bits first.'

'You *are* crazy.'

8

RIGHT FROM THE BEGINNING she has known that she is incapable of being absorbed into a form for which a few missing nubbins of flesh are the defining point – but her fear has been too heavy to allow thoughts of escape to ascend. She thinks of Marina Beach, the soft sand underfoot, the perpetual motion of the waves and the task at hand seems as immense as the sea. Will she ever have the courage to swim against the tide of detestable continuance? She can hear the wind outside trying to imitate the sound of the sea. Even the wind cannot distract her thoughts. She misses her old friends in the village terribly. Will they still be in the old village? Can she recognize them after twelve years? With the obsession to escape comes a sort of despair. She outwardly tries to keep her balance, but inside she is at boiling point. She must find her old friends again.

This morning, she is just about to have breakfast. She walks down the stairs; her red sari rustles as she descends. 'Eunuch, eunuch,' the folds of her nylon sari seem to whisper.

People say a man is an island and needs to be left alone. A man's heart needs to beat to the tune of the tide, they say. People say that a woman is like a tree. From her womb grows the family tree. What of the eunuch? Ramani thinks. Eunuchs have no identity; zombies with no identity and no options. There are a million eunuchs in India, making a living by dancing at weddings (or being paid to leave the premises), turning up at births unannounced and threatening to curse the baby boy (unless paid off), or as prostitutes. All these options make her feel revulsion and despair. People in the village used to say that life is like the Kaveri River, with ever-changing rhythms and relentless passage until it reaches the sea. She thinks eunuchs are like weeds – catching debris from the river of life; a combination of stagnation and decay. The river of life will flow through the weeds, until life is renewed again in the sea.

Nobody here will change anything, she thinks. She will have to change things herself. At breakfast, she says nothing. She is surprised at the increasing vehemence of her thoughts of freedom.

Mira is sitting at her usual place at the table for breakfast. She has powdered her face and lined her eyelids with thick coats of *mai*. It is as if she has resolved to hide her recovery from the physical injuries, reject the fact that the bruises are fading around her eyes. A eunuch with blemishes will always be a eunuch with black and blue marks, even if a mirror can no longer recreate her battered image.

Mira has cooked breakfast today. She has made masala dosais. She has not cooked for some time, and the masala stuffing the paper-thin dosais looks a bit runny. Mira looks as though after all the injury, despair and weariness, she is finally triumphing. Mira gazes at Ramani with a surge of tenderness. 'I was waiting for you,' she says. 'Breakfast is not the same without you.'

Rajinder is away for three days. She has travelled across the border into Kerala to bring more videos for the shop. A new shipment of smuggled porn videos has arrived from Dubai. By the time she comes back, I will be free. My real life will begin, Ramani thinks.

Kamalam has already gone to the clinic. Through the window she can see couples lining up outside the clinic's door. Kamalam will not be back until late. Ramani wonders if she should tell Mira the truth. She should perhaps tell her, and ask her to keep her escape a secret. But in her present state of exhaustion, she might not resist telling the truth, she thinks. Ramani knows that she will need to leave right away. That will give her a three-day headstart before

Rajinder returns. Kamalam is unlikely to go after her without Rajinder.

Thoughts of escape swarm her head; she keeps repeating the word 'escape' in her mind to rob it of its terror. She observes Mira eating breakfast in a detached state, and decides to sacrifice any loyalty to Mira for her own happiness.

Mira stands up and gives her a hug. 'Ramani, you've got to go. I know what you are thinking. I also know you don't belong here. Rajinder will never be able to keep you night and day anyway.'

Ramani is stunned. She must have let panic show on her face. She chides herself for her rashness.

Mira brings her a pink salwar kameez. Mira is the one with the pretty clothes. She is the only one allowed to wear fashionable clothes. The rest of the eunuchs wear a red sari. As is customary with eunuchs, the folds of the sari are tucked in at the back in a characteristic manner.

'I stole this from a shop for you,' she says. 'I knew it would come in handy one day. You are pretty. Put this on and put on this make-up. You'll pass off as a pretty young woman.' Here her voice breaks off. 'Go,' she says. 'Go quickly, before I change my mind.' She gives Ramani two hundred rupees which she has squirrelled away under her mattress. That is what sisters are for, Ramani thinks.

Ramani lays a hand on Mira's shoulder and they hug. Then Mira closes the door after Ramani, tears streaming down her face.

Ramani is surprised at how cool it is outside. The sea has woken up early. She sees policemen in the road ahead. She wonders if she must ask them for help. She decides against it. That might be foolish. She must take no chances. Ramani realizes that from her experiences with danger and living in a harem, she is now incredibly alert to the scent of misfortune. I am like a wild animal, she thinks.

She wonders where she must go. She decides to go to the bus station. She must run far away from Madras, so Rajinder cannot find her. She plans to take a bus to Bangalore. She walks briskly, then breaks into a run.

Any attempt to reconstruct a life needs a good design; like building a new house. The more one faces a terrible reality, the stronger is the intention to right things. It seems that the Lord Ganesha has given Ramani the strength to escape from non-existence. She runs for a long time. She must have run over twenty miles, she thinks.

She reaches a large open ground – a playground of sorts. She sees children playing cricket in different parts of the ground. She sees some spectators clapping hands. It must be a school cricket game, she thinks. She sees some kites fluttering in the distance. The kites flutter like dancers, stamping their feet and whirling around in the blue sky. She sees these dancers soar into whirlwinds and turn around quickly to slice, to break other kites. It is a kite competition! she thinks. I wonder if my hands still remember. She feels her heart flutter.

Ramani sees a man holding some kind of ticket. 'What's going on?'

'There is a kite competition here. You can watch if you want. There is a prize of five hundred rupees to the winner. It is a fight until the death for the kites,' he says.

'I'm game,' she replies.

'Women cannot fly kites,' he says. 'Look, it says so in the rules of the competition.'

'I am not a woman. I am a eunuch,' she says.

'Who are you kidding?' he sneers. 'As if I cannot make out a eunuch; they stand out like an abomination, a scar.' Then he concedes, 'All right, you can enter if you wish to be humiliated.'

Ramani rushes to the shop to buy some bright red paper. She must make a kite quickly. She cuts the paper into a diamond. She sticks the red paper onto the frame. She designs her kite hastily.

The kite stares at her from the table, next to the rope. The sun is descending, almost against her will. She looks at the kite with its shiny red coat. Her kite is a devilish diamond of hope; her only hope. Ramani, take it.

With purposeful intent, she fixes the rope. Now for the manja, she thinks. She picks up some dog shit and puts it in a plastic bag. She then smashes a milk bottle and starts mixing the manja. Slowly her hands shift into a rhythm. She closes her nose to the smell of the manja. She throws off the excess manja, like a warrior throwing off excess armour before a battle. Too much manja will slow the kite down, she thinks. Ramani feels an intoxication, the familiar rhythm of the kite in her blood. The kite bucks like a bull.

Kites light up the sky; but they never drive wind away. Wind is like the oil which illuminates the kites. She sees her kite moving in the sky with other kites to keep it company. She is so engrossed in flying her kite that she does not hear the man.

'Name of kite?' he bellows.

'Oh, sorry – *China Moon*,' she says, impulsively.

'There is already another *China Moon*,' he says.

'You can be *China Sun*.'

The spectators cannot wait and start clapping their hands, as if heralding the onset of a cosmic dance. The whole neighbourhood comes out to watch. Ramani has tears in her eyes. She is free!

The clapping becomes faster, continuing to draw the dance out of the tune. The man next to Ramani reaches up high, his back taut as he pulls on his kite to change direction at the last minute. His kite quenches his thirst for battle by slicing into her kite. But the trusted nai pee manja does its trick. Ramani holds her kite firm and steady. His kite loses its head. 'She's good!' someone calls out.

The other kites stamp their hooves across the sky and dance and whirl. One by one, they stop spinning, as a hierarchical order is established. One by one, the dancers drop out and the kites seem to move of their own accord. The competitors concentrate hard, intent on subduing the enemy with the power of their manja.

One by one, kites fall. *India Ink* is gone; *Madras Madman* is gone; *Veerapandya Kattabomman* is gone; *Bangalore Buffalo* is gone; *Tanjore Doll* is gone. There is no malicious intent. A storm of applause breaks out as each kite flyer takes his bow, retrieves his kite and acknowledges the enemy. This is tame compared to the competitions in Salem, Ramani thinks.

'The girl is still winning!' someone yells. Ramani does not hear the voice. Her ears are tuned to hear the whispers of the wind: *o-shush o-shush*, the wind says. One careless move is all it takes, she thinks, as her kite strains to listen to the wind. The wind picks up. The sea seems to be huffing and puffing hard. The only thing a kite needs to fly is a dream. Dreams can climb above trees and clouds. Ramani feels her kite muscles become taut. She tries to loosen her grip on the rope.

It is important to relax and to deliver that message via the rope to the kite, almost telephonically. Don't worry, *China Sun*, relax. You have the open sky and cool sea breeze. I'll make the moves and I promise not to startle you, she thinks.

Kumar moves his kite southwards. The north wind is treacherous, he thinks. I must avoid it. His *China Moon* flies proudly. Father used to say that kite flying is a not an easy skill to pass down generations. A child does not necessarily inherit the skill of kite flying. But once you can reel a kite properly, you never lose the skill. He thinks he is now better than his father.

Kumar sees a girl making a 'five-point turn'. That is a move he used to practise many years ago. The crowd is unsure what the girl is doing, but Kumar knows right away. She is trying to move her kite away from the north wind, all the while with her back to him; so that she can ambush me, he thinks. He feels respect for the girl. Even Lakshmi can't fly a kite as craftily as this, he thinks.

He moves closer to the girl. He is not going to let her pass him. She veers to the right, and he follows. Like sailing a boat: tack for tack and gybe for gybe. This girl is good, he thinks. Still, let's see who beats whom. He deliberately does not pull his kite in close. She could slam on the brakes and ram into his kite. He sees the manja glisten on her rope. What kind of manja has she got? Surely, she cannot have glass on her manja? A girl would not be so bold. He has never come across another kite flyer with an even coating of glass. She must have glued it on, he thinks. That will make her rope far too heavy. Not like my nai pee manja. Pound for pound, dog shit is far lighter than glue.

The crowd hovers closer, now more interested. 'See, I told you we must allow more girls in the competition,' the ticket collector screams in delight. Market forces have made him change his tune.

Kumar speeds up his movements, his muscles straining hard. The girl speeds up as well, matching him. He slows down and she slows down.

Enough of this joking around, he thinks. I have to finish her off.

His thoughts are interrupted by the ticket collector. The sun is almost asleep.

'We shall adjourn for the night. Both of you get two hundred rupees. Tomorrow the winner will get three hundred!'

Kumar nods and sets off for home, tucking *China Moon* safely under his arm.

'Is it really three hundred rupees tomorrow?' Ramani asks the ticket collector.

'Sure – you made my ticket sales go up. People will come back tomorrow. That's why I stopped the match today. More sales tomorrow,' he beams.

Three hundred rupees! Ramani thinks. Enough to make her stay here for the night. She has no fear of nightfall or darkness. She will still have two nights before Rajinder returns to Madras. She holds *China Sun* in her arms carefully. Tomorrow the two red kites will fight to the death, she thinks. She says a silent prayer to Lord Ganesha.

Rajinder has cut short her trip and is on her way home. With the intuition of a mother, she knows something is wrong. On the bus journey back it is raining. Then the rain stops. Rajinder sees raindrops suspended on the windows of her bus. She sees a big rainbow. It is an incomplete rainbow. That isn't unusual. But this rainbow has the red and orange missing. She knows it means bad luck. She hopes there has been no trouble. It is Ramani, she intuits.

She rushes through the front door. She sees Mira sitting quietly in a corner. 'Where is Ramani?' she demands.

'I think she went with Kamalam,' Mira lies. Rajinder knows Mira is lying. Something in her heart tells her that Ramani has gone.

'Has she run away?' she asks.

Mira is silent.

'All I want to know is – did she want to go, or did something make her?'

If her mind is made up, then I must not stop her, she thinks. She feels a sadness descend on her shoulders, and it weighs her down like the heavy pallu of a sari.

She leaves the harem quickly. She goes to the Ganesha temple nearby. Lord Ganesha understands eunuchs. He understands the violence of their birth. After all, he was born of the same violence – an elephant head replaced his own after his father had severed it. She wonders if Lord Ganesha will listen to her prayers. She knows he has always listened to her. She walks up to the altar, bows before the deity of Ganesha and holds her hands over the sacred fire. She does this three times.

The pujari of the temple nods to her in acquaintance. 'What did you pray for?' he asks.

'That Ganesha will protect my daughter Ramani, look after her and make her happy. That she will succeed in the battles she will face in life.' Her eyes fill with tears.

The priest looks at her, still holding the tray with the sacred fire and the *prasadam*, the offering especially prepared for the gods. The flame flickers at Rajinder, but her tears ignore the flame. Rajinder picks at the *prasadam*, accepts the blessing and puts it in her mouth, in communion.

'I hope I have done the right thing with Ramani,' she prays.

The pujari wipes her tears. He looks at the eunuch, her tear-stained face and her robust frame. He knows Lord Ganesha will feel her pain.

The eunuch cuts a forlorn figure as she walks home.

Back at home, Kumar exclaims, 'Boy! That was some competition! I was a bit rusty. I am in the finals, though. My hands are all chafed.'

'Give me a look.' Lakshmi holds his palms. She studies the lines on his right palm. 'Your palm says you have stubbornness and a will to win,' she says.

'What else does it say?'

'That you were born to cure sadness and build happiness.'

'And?'

'That you are lucky and that you will live long.'

'Lakshmi, I know I am lucky – I have *you* here with me. I just wish I could make you walk again.'

'Don't worry. Everything below my waist is dying, getting rotten and numb. Even Lord Ganesha can't fix me,' she replies.

It makes him angry, the fact that she cannot walk or run. He holds her toes. They are curled up on the footrest of the wheelchair. He prises them open with his fingers and rubs her feet, trying to restore some feeling and warmth. Her feet have the coldness of stone.

Most nights she just sleeps in her wheelchair and some nights he carries her into his bed. He covers her with a sheet as she falls asleep. Tonight she is leaning over to one side, her body bunched up to the right. She looks like she is going to fall off the edge of her wheelchair. He pretends she is falling off, and holds her tight to keep her safe. Lakshmi tries to sleep but she can't. She closes her eyes as if she is sleeping, and gently lifts the bedsheet and covers both of them. He moves slightly. He must be uncomfortable sleeping next to me, she thinks. He breathes hard at times. He talks at night. The more he dreams, the more he talks, she thinks. She talks too, but on the inside. She says, 'I love you, you crazy kite flyer.'

When he opens his eyes, it is almost morning. He has been sitting with her and holding her close all night. He goes back to his bed for a short while before the sun comes up.

She wakes first. 'Hey, kite flyer,' she says. 'Ready for your battle?'

'Of course,' he smiles groggily. 'There is this girl in the competition. She is in the finals, too.'

'You'll be way too cunning for her.'

Back at the ground, Kumar takes up his marked position. An expectant crowd has gathered. The girl has also taken her position, again with her back to him.

'She is really pretty,' he hears a woman exclaim.

The kites ascend to the trees. Kumar's kite goes up higher than the palm tree nearby. He sees the girl's kite ascend, its rope getting twisted.

Ramani lets her kite free, and it slowly gains height. She deliberately lets her rope twist. After all, who cares if a tree has mangled branches, as long as it grows to a great height? It will make her manja stronger.

The palm tree leaves sway slightly. The sea is still asleep and the branches rustle here and there. The tips of the pointed leaves have a lighter tinge. Like henna highlights in Mira's hair, Ramani thinks.

The ground is already warm beneath her feet. In the corner of the ground, near the palm trees, frogs seek refuge in the stagnant water.

She moves slightly and shifts her grip as the wind begins to pick up. She now has her kite between the palm trees, with the breeze blowing between them. Like the Kaveri River, she thinks. She needs to focus on the currents; what were they called, Eddy? She focuses on each whorl and waits for the time to move her kite towards her opponent's kite.

She feels a force within her, a powerful impulse. She takes small steps, impelled by the need to prove her mettle in this battle.

Kumar moves quickly through his routine. Enough of all this manoeuvring, he thinks. Girls waste a lot of time and energy.

It is time for the end game.

He reels his kite in, sharply angling it towards the girl. Glass crunches glass. What? The girl must have thick glass on her manja! How has she managed to keep the glass coat so even?

The escape

He can see what she has done. Twisting her rope has made her rope tauter than his. He attacks again. Glass crunches glass again, and they both move their feet as some glass falls underfoot. With excruciating slowness, he sees his rope begin to chafe. All this whirling and swirling has made the rope frazzled and almost translucent.

He is powerless to do anything. The rope stays briefly still and then, bit by bit, it parts as his kite begins to fall.

The crowd bursts into applause. Kumar does not smile. He still cannot believe he has been beaten. He remembers seeing an English movie at the only cinema in town showing English movies. It was a cowboy picture. He remembers a cowboy saying after a duel, 'However fast you are, there is always a faster man.' Or a woman, he thinks ruefully.

He is filled with an admiration for this girl. He sees her accepting the three hundred rupees. Horns blow in the crowd and a few men empty bottles of arrack. 'Drink! Drink! Drink!' they chant.

Kumar walks over to the girl. She turns. Kumar thinks he has seen this girl before. He knows her from somewhere, but his memory fails him. His brain seems to have swept aside his memory of this girl like a damp kite in the Kaveri River wind.

There is an awkward and prolonged silence as they regard each other, searching for clues.

Ramani thinks this young man seems familiar too. But she knows she cannot afford to trust anyone here. And she has no time to lose. Rajinder will be coming back in two days and is sure to come after her.

'What manja did you use?' Kumar asks. He wonders if she will share her secret.

'Dog shit and glass: *nai pee manja*,' she smiles candidly. Her mouth curls up on one side, like a hockey stick.

Her smile gives her away. 'Raman?'

'Hey, kite flyer,' she says. She looks at his curly hair, now speckled with grey.

Kumar furrows his brow quizzically, looking at her female attire.

'I am Ramani now,' she says.

The good thing about old friendships is that there is always plenty of time for answers later on. Old friendships are a tunnel into our past. No one should ask questions in a tunnel. Tunnels echo too much.

'Listen,' Kumar says excitedly. 'Lakshmi's at home. We got married.'

Blinded by their affection, they begin to run back down the tunnel of childhood friendships, their hearts pounding. 'Twelve years!' they exclaim as they run.

Twelve years!

They run faster, madly, deliriously, and each step takes them into an infinite timeless realm; neither winning nor losing, life nor death can separate them again.

In the school at KKP, Gowrie teacher used to say that the three of them were like particles in an atom: Proton, Neutron and Electron; inseparable – a trio of particles in an atomic flood.

'Let's go and meet Electron!' they shout.

Back at home, Electron fidgets in her wheelchair, waiting for Kumar to return.

9

I CAN FEEL the humidity of Madras on my skin.
The barren sunny sky tries to conjure up a rain cloud.
I am in a cycle rickshaw. I sit on a cushioned seat,
covered with a canopy hood. The rickshaw man
pedals the cycle, driving the three-wheeled
contraption forwards.

It is time for my monthly haircut. I am on my
way to Cool Cut.

'Where have you been?' Kumar says. 'I haven't
seen you here for a long time.'

'I've been travelling a lot as a journalist,' I say.

For the past few years I have carried on the
business of being a journalist. My professor at Madras
University's journalism school says that as a
journalist I must learn to recognize the truth. The
truth has many faces, and often wears masks, he says.
I have found that truth can be found behind long
faces, short faces, sad faces, smiling faces – and dead
faces.

Many of the regulars are sitting there, waiting

for their turn. As usual, Cool Cut is a hotbed of political discussion.

I look up at the familiar portrait of MGR staring down at me. Years have passed, but MGR is still the chief minister. I look for the familiar kite on the wall. The frame is no longer in place.

'You used to have a kite here,' I say.

'Yes,' Kumar says. 'It's a long story. I have begun flying it again. So tell me what stories you have covered as a journalist. This young man is a journalist and an old client of mine,' Kumar introduces me to the rest of the patrons.

This is the paradox of journalism. If it is all about uncovering the truth, then why are newspaper articles called 'stories'? Sometimes I have found that truth can be like one of those Russian dolls. You know the ones I mean, the ones with sequentially smaller dolls inside larger ones. Sometimes you have to open many dolls before you find the real one.

'I have tracked the secret training camps for the LTTE being run by the Indian government,' I tell him.

'Wow! I've heard rumours, but wasn't sure if that was true.'

MGR was born in Kandy in Sri Lanka, although his parents were from Kerala. The pulse of the people beats in MGR's veins, I say. That is why he is not just a politician, but a phenomenon. But you knew that already, I tell Kumar. When MGR realizes that people here will live and die for the Tamil language, he persuades the central government to secretly train Tamil Tiger guerrillas in the forests around Sathyamangalam. Tamils here feel the anger of the Tamils in Sri Lanka. They may not like the Sri Lankan Tamils, and their bastardized language, but the language binds them together. It is said that blood is thicker than water, but a language is much thicker; it cannot flow through blood vessels – it needs to roll off tongues.

'The Sri Lankans have really ruined Tamil. Their Tamil is so different, I can hardly understand it,' Kumar says. 'I have a Sri Lankan Tamil customer and he always asks me if he can fellate his cigarette in my shop!' We laugh.

Supporting terrorists never works for a government, I continue. People who are driven by religion or language have the passion of tigers. They do not fear death. And trainers always want to retain control of the beast, for their own political ends. In the long run, the trainers will find that they will never be able to control the beast. The Americans are training Islamic guerrillas against the Russians in northern Pakistan. The Indian government will learn a bitter lesson in Sri Lanka, as will the Americans in

Afghanistan. The central government has made a mistake in giving in to MGR's fevered support for the Tamil Tiger guerrillas. The Tigers will never be able to share power in a democratic manner. Already, in Tiger-controlled territories in Sri Lanka, a child is being taken from each family to join their army of suicide bombers.

Kumar listens intently. He looks at the clock. 'I'd better stop talking and get back to work,' he says.

We talk of things big and small, as I wait for my haircut. I look around the salon. Now there are three chairs!

'You've expanded,' I say aloud.

'That's my new barber,' he says.

'But, she's a . . . she's a . . .'

'. . . girl?'

It is unusual to have a female barber in Madras. Women here never even enter a barber shop.

'I'll just wait until you are free,' I stammer.

'I am being progressive,' he says. 'At Cool Cut we have always been ahead of the times. I was the first shop in Madras to have air conditioning. The kadallaikaran in my old village used to say that there are many female haircutters and male cooks in English-speaking countries. Here, in Tamil Nadu, it is the opposite.'

I see a little man with a protuberant paunch lean

back in one of the padded red chairs, his arms folded behind his head. He remains perfectly still, and makes no remonstrance as the barber in chair no. 2 smoothes lather on his armpits. Then the barber begins to shave his armpit. Every now and then, as if overcome by the odour, he looks away and breathes deeply.

The girl barber is taking a break. She is in charge of chair no. 3. She sits on one of the desks in the back room, swinging her legs. Her face is animated and pretty, and none of the men in Cool Cut are able to take their eyes off her. She wears a bright yellow salwar kameez. My eyes catch hers in the mirror and she winks at me. I lower my eyes quickly, unaccustomed to such familiarity.

The next month, I return to Cool Cut for another haircut.

Today Madras seems not so much asleep, but choked and locked in sadness. MGR has had a stroke and has been transferred to a hospital in America. The prime minister of the country had sent a private aircraft for MGR to be flown to America for treatment.

Cool Cut has been a veritable temple to MGR. It overlooks silent streets and empty buses. People are afraid to board the city buses lest they be burned down by grieving mobs.

At every street corner stands a group of rickshaw pullers. Their rickshaws, idle beasts of metal and rubber, stand with their canopies folded. After all, had MGR not given them chappals to wear on their bare feet? MGR was the master of such populist generosity. A few years ago, when he had taken over as chief minister of the state, he had announced that government schools would provide free lunches to students. With him in power, there *were* things such as free lunches after all.

At the seashore stand fishermen, looking distraught, their nets tied in the middle with red sashes. There will be no nets cast that day. Who else will insist on the completion of government housing for the fishermen?

The Tamil Tigers begin eliminating other Sri Lankan Tamil groups, who are fighting for the same cause in Sri Lanka. Their leader, Prabhakaran, believes that there must be only one group in control. He developed this theory while training alongside the PLO, IRA and the Hizbollah in Lebanon. Now his cadres train in the jungles of Tamil Nadu, supported by MGR's government. Leaders of other Tamil terrorist organizations are 'rubber-necked', one by one – decapitated by burning rubber tyres around their necks. While MGR was around, they always had his ear. It is time to consolidate the future, they reckon.

MGR's illness has rendered the city folk susceptible to long silences and deathlike stupor. Even an occasional DMK party member does not dare to relieve the tedium with joyous expression.

Kumar greets me with a mournful expression on his face. He has the radio set to his usual station and we listen to live commentary on the state of MGR's health from America. The radio announces that twenty-two people have killed themselves in Madras: eleven men, ten women and one eunuch.

'Bloody alis – eunuchs – always kidnapping kids and making a nuisance of themselves at weddings!' I say.

'Well. Society has always had eunuchs; if they do not adopt kids, who will look after them in their old age? After all, a eunuch does not choose to be a eunuch. Every eunuch has been taken from a family,' the girl barber says. She is right, I guess. But her question makes me think. Do I detect a trace of vehemence in her voice?

Many people have died today. They have died in the hope that their death will be a sacrifice to the gods to save MGR's life. In life he had a kill ratio of two for every political rally. Now, nearing death, his kill ratio has risen to twenty-two. 'MGR is dying,' Kumar says.

'I forgot to tell you about his rally I attended,

many years ago. He mesmerized the audience, even with that gravelly voice of his,' I say.

'His voice became like that only after he was shot in the throat by M.R. Radha, that good-for-nothing actor,' Kumar replies.

Outside, lines form next to the public hospital. People demand to donate blood for MGR. '*Rathathin rathame!*' ('Blood of blood!'), they yell, remembering his rallying call. In the beginning, a few doctors try to reason with the crowd. They point out the difficulty in transporting the blood to America; why, the Americans might have enough blood.

'It is *not* Tamil blood!' the people scream and begin to pelt rocks. The superintendent of the hospital quickly agrees to collect the blood. In his illness, MGR has done the blood bank a good turn. The blood stockpile will last for two years.

While MGR's fate hangs in the balance, the crowd waits patiently in a line, wearing the chappals he has given them. They pray to no one other than this all-but-extinguished star.

Most of the customers at Cool Cut begin to leave, some head for the hospital to join the queues. Kumar makes a sign suggesting that he might have a sit-down for a while. I can tell his heart is not in his job today.

It is all very well, I think, somewhat selfishly.

Now I will have to have the girl barber. She is pretty, and considerate. I am sure she means well. Women are generally like that. They mean well. But I can't count on her to cut my hair properly; especially not in the front.

There is a sense of dubiety as I lean back in the plush red chair. The girl barber sprays my hair with water. She leans my head backwards into a bowl. 'I am going to wash your hair first,' she says.

'Kumar never washes my hair,' I protest.

'Stop being so nervous,' she says. 'When you are with Kumar, let him cut his way. When you are with me, let me cut *my* way,' she says. She smiles as if I have reminded her about something. She runs warm water through my hair and begins to massage my scalp.

How can I forget the sensation? I am condemned to the feminine touch. From this moment, I am prepared to let go of my old familiar certainties and sink into wanton pleasure. There is a faint air of helplessness. The sensation is delicious as her soft hands caress my scalp. Why is my defence crumbling? I know that this is her tactic of persuasion, a sales pitch. From now on, every haircutting experience is going to be edged with incompleteness.

Her fingers move the hair away from my forehead. 'Just relax,' she says. Then I hear the snip-snip of scissors. I feel my hair part like paddy fields in the wind. I can see her reflection in the mirror in front of us. The closeness of our bodies while she cuts my hair appears strangely symbiotic in the reflection. Her eyes seem to look into the mirror beyond me, as if she is looking into the distance. Then I hear footsteps cross the floor. She comes back, brandishing a mirror to show me the back of my head. 'That cut all right?' she asks.

Her feminine touch has made me feel all woozy. I don't care how my hair looks now; my hair may as well be blonde, like those foreign film stars. She has had complete freedom over my hair. An artist needs that freedom of expression, I think.

I reach home. As I enter the door, I brush my hair with my fingers, lost in thought. Mother comes out and says, 'Your hair looks good. For the first time, it is not too short in the front.'

I tell my mother about the female barber. 'She has soft hands, and flawless skin. When she cleanses my hair it feels so good. She even rubbed my scalp with coconut oil!'

Dad walks in, shaking his head, 'Female barber? Next that fellow at Cool Cut will be hiring hookers.'

Back at the video shop, Rajinder waves her hand and the policeman enters for his monthly visit. He begins with his usual 'vice squad' routine of checking for porn videos.

'What have you got for me regarding my daughter?' she asks.

'Ramani? Well, she seems happy. She is working as a barber in Cool Cut.'

'Does she need anything?'

'Not that I can see. That Kumar fellow seems to care for her. He treats her not just as a friend, but as family.'

Rajinder smiles. She is pleased. She slips the policeman a hundred-rupee note. 'Just make sure she is all right, and take care of anyone troubling her. Each month I will give you this note to protect her.'

'And she is not to know about this protection money?'

'She must never know that I know where she lives, or that you are following her. Tell me more about this Kumar fellow and where they live.'

'The barber shop owner, Kumar, he has a crippled wife. I think they all live near the shop. The poor woman is paralysed below the waist.'

Later, at the dinner table, Rajinder lets Mira and Kamalam know about Ramani.

'Is she happy?' asks Mira excitedly.

'Yes, my girl.'

'I'm glad. I miss her, though.'

'We *all* miss her.'

Kamalam is deep in thought. Then she excuses herself. She has been healing people in need for years. Now a young lady needs her.

St. Thomas Mount in Madras is well known; it is said that Thomas, Jesus's disciple, made his way there and eventually died on the Mount. However, very few people know of the Kali temple that exists there.

Goddess Kali in all her bloodthirsty fury looks down at Kamalam. There are four fires blazing in the temple, one from each of Goddess Kali's four arms. The flames from these fires rise high, direct to the spirits of the eunuchs. These fires are lit to send messages to the eunuch spirits.

Kamalam stays there and prays for a whole day. During the day, no sound, food, or water passes her lips. *Kali* translates as 'time' and the Goddess Kali is capable of devouring time and turning back the clock.

Back at Cool Cut, Kumar and Ramani are finishing for the day. Lakshmi waits for them upstairs. She wishes she could walk down to Cool Cut. She sighs. Her feet and legs have been like dead wood for years.

Then she thinks she feels a sudden warmth in her feet. First she thinks she might have spilt oil on her feet while cooking. It shouldn't make a difference, she thinks; I can't feel a burn anyway. She looks down at her feet. A faint blush appears on her foot. It seems a beautiful sight to see colour in pale, hard, lifeless skin. An excited charm lights up her face, as colour seems to slowly spread to her toes. She must be mistaken. It must be her imagination. She strokes her leg and is surprised that she can feel her touch, albeit faintly. 'Kumar! Ramani!' she screams. They do not hear her. They are busy at work.

Back at the temple, Kamalam has finished her fast. She is weary. She has neither eaten nor spoken for a day. She looks up at Goddess Kali. 'You don't have to say anything. Thank you,' she says. It is almost evening. It is time to go home.

I am on my way to Cool Cut. A lot has happened since my last visit here. MGR has been taken from this earth. I wonder if he misses his 'blood of blood'. I wonder if he can see people standing by his embalmed body and saying goodbye. His wife, Janaki, and his mistress, Jayalalitha, are both there, regarding each other with disdain. Each is surrounded by a band of politicians, plotting for power.

I wonder how it will be on his final journey. Will the Madras city lights flash by, the streets filled with mourners shouting 'Puratchi thalaiver is no more'? As he flashes by like lightning, does he see the sea? The sea water glimmering in the moonlight? Or the low wall of the drive-in where lovers have congregated to see his movies? Or the headlines in the newspaper, detailing the chief minister's funeral: *his* funeral?

I think he will not forget this dusty, polluted and humid city, the incessant noise, the throng of fishermen. Perhaps he will see the politicians arriving for his funeral in luxurious pleasure cars; men and women carrying the flag of his party and posters with his portraits; Tamil Tiger guerrillas wrapping his portrait in a blood-stained military tablecloth, having eliminated the leaders of all the other Sri Lankan Tamil groups.

He will see his wife and his mistress fight for political power. It no longer matters whom he prefers. His people now have the choice. Will they vote for his wife Janaki, even though he had originally 'won' her in a card game from a well-known gambler? Or will they prefer his mistress Jayalalitha, his co-star in many of his movies?

He now feels no tug, no conflict of interest, no shame and no guilt. He sees himself as a tree, standing calmly and talking in a low tone, as his wife and mistress sit on each side. He hears a rustling amongst the clouds as people's dreams ascend, crowding the limited cirrus. He looks down and sees hundreds of nameless children, writing of their love for him on the wall of his house.

The wall of his house glows a bright red as the sun sets in Madras. There is a sound of a veena playing around him. MGR listens to the song. It is not in Tamil. It is in an unknown tongue. 'Farewell, sunset and shadows of my Tamil country. Farewell, my people, my blood of blood, rathathin rathame.'

I have almost reached Cool Cut. It is that time of the month again. Something looks different about the building. First, I think it is the advertisements stuck on the wall; maybe the shoes lined up outside the salon have made it look different. Then I realize the building is taller. Kumar, Lakshmi and Ramani have built an apartment above Cool Cut. It has a terrace on the top which looks out at the sea, over the rooftops behind. It has three windows looking out to the road, where I am walking. I see the shadows of three kites flying out of the windows. I try to jump and hold onto the shadows with all my might, hoping they will carry me to the clouds. I jump as high as I can until the power of three overcomes me. I see they have thrown the shadows so high that I can't catch them. The shadows fly, hugging each other joyously. I hear laughter, and happy voices. The laughter, it is in Tamil. The voices, they are in the language of love. The kite flyers laugh loud, and the laughter is transmitted telephonically along the kite ropes to rest amongst the clouds above Madras.

The mistress won the battle after all. Jayalalitha eventually became chief minister of Tamil Nadu, while Janaki disappeared into obscurity. Her reign has been marred by accusations of corruption and nepotism.

She even has a road named after her in Chicago: Dr. J. Jayalalitha Way. Location: Devon and Broadway, Chicago.

Jayalalitha served as Chief Minister until the DMK came back to power led by the wily veteran, Karunanidhi, who is now the chief minister of Tamil Nadu.

Dr. Karunanidhi is well known for his oratory skills and proficiency as a Tamil playwright.

I asked Lakshmi if she would share her recipe for her famous burfi with my readers. She tells me she now owns a microwave and has adapted her recipe for modern lifestyles.

Lakshmi's Burfi
Ingredients
1 cup sugar
3 cups milk powder (for chocolate burfi, add ⅓ cup of cocoa powder)
300 ml full cream
½ cup chopped almonds or pistachio nuts
1 teaspoon of saffron

Mix the sugar, milk powder and full cream in a bowl and microwave for four minutes (she uses a 750w microwave). Add the saffron and ¼ cup of the nuts to the mixture, stir and microwave for a further two minutes.

Allow to cool and cut into cubes. Garnish with the remaining chopped pistachio or almond nuts and serve.